INTERVIEWING GOD

I.Y. WADE

i

INTERVIEWING GOD

Limits of Liability and Disclaimer of Warranty

Warning – Disclaimer

All scripture and verses are taken from the New World Translation Bible and the Koran.

Cover Design: Oniel De La Cruz – Designs on the Fly

Interior Design: Shavonna Bush – All Write Editing
Editor: Shavonna Bush – All Write Editing

I.Y. Wade
166publishing@gmail.com
166publishing.com

Printed in the United States of America
First Printing, 2018
ISBN 978-1-5136-3426-5

𝔄cknowledgments

I'd like to give thanks to our Father who art in Heaven and to Christ the Messiah, for through them all things are possible.

To my family, friends, and the readers who have supported me and given me the encouragement to continue, thank you, thank you, and thank you!

Finally, to my son; the wind beneath my wings, you make me a better man. I love you more than life!

I.Y. Wade

Prologue

John heard the door slam. His father was returning from another day of looking for work. Maybe today would be the day that he found something. The day he wouldn't come home drunk, or high on methamphetamine. It was almost two years since he had lost his job at the Boeing plant due to downsizing. 9/11 had changed so many things. A lot of good, hardworking people had lost everything: their jobs, their homes, their life savings, and any medical coverage they had. Times were tough, to say the least.

John's mother did what she usually did when his father came home in the early evening.

"Hey, honey. How was your day?" she asked going to give him a peck on the cheek.

John's father sneered, ignoring her.

"What's for dinner, woman?"

John could hear his mother reply nervously, "I-I made smothered pork chops, string beans, and rice pilaf with mushrooms sweetie."

She had good reason to be nervous. She could smell the alcohol on his breath. Although theirs was a dry county, John's father always found a way to get liquor.

"You stupid cow! How many times do I have to tell you I don't like my chops smothered."

His mother had made smothered pork chops plenty of times, and he had eaten them plenty of times, but this was today's excuse to berate and beat her.

When John heard his father slap his mother he did what his mother had taught him to do whenever his father became irate. He closed his bedroom door, ran into the closet and crouched down on the floor. John's mother did the best she could to protect John from his father's wrath. The last time ten-year-old John tried to intervene, his father gave him a black eye and nearly broke his arm. The police took him down to the county jail for a day and released him as long as he promised he would get into "AA" and seek counseling. After all, they lived in a small county in Clay Center Kansas, a place where everyone knew everyone else. The local police looked at such things as issues that could be handled between husband and wife. John could hear his mother screaming, but there would be no one coming to her rescue. The nearest neighbor lived an acre and a half down the road.

His mother had also taught him to recite the "Lord's Prayer" whenever he felt scared, or in danger. He covered his ears and began to say the words that have given him and multitudes of the distraught solace in times of trouble.

"Our Father who art in heaven Hallowed be thy name. Thy kingdom come. Thy will be done on Earth, As it is in Heaven. Give us this day our daily bread. Forgive us our sins, as we forgive those who sin against us. Lead us not into temptation, But deliver us from evil…"

John spoke words that had little meaning to him.

He had no understanding of temptation or evil. He could only grasp that his dad was bad to him and his mom.

"For thine is the kingdom, the power, and the glory. For ever and ever. Amen."

John lay there for hours until he fell asleep.

The next morning he was awakened by the sound of police radios. The neighbors had called 911 twenty minutes earlier and reported hearing a single gunshot coming from their neighbor's home.

"Ah, yes, dispatch, this is Sheriff Wayne over at the McKinneth residence. We're going to need a vehicle over here to pick up two."

His deputy followed him with his flashlight bright in the dimness of the morning's first light. As the two troopers walked through the home, the deputy's flashlight reflected off of a wedding picture on a mantle in the living room. The caption read *Happy twelfth wedding anniversary to Mr. and Mrs. Kyle and Lynn McKinneth.*

The deputy made an off the cuff, inappropriate remark, "I thought thirteen was supposed to be unlucky."

The Sherriff put his finger up to his lips, "Quiet Carson."

He had heard a noise coming from the bedroom on the right. He drew his weapon and slowly opened the door. Standing there wide-eyed was John, hungry, and terrified.

"Where's my mom and dad?" he asked.

The sheriff answered, "They're all right son. Just come with me. Everything is going to be fine."

As they walked through the house, the sheriff covered the young boy's face so he wouldn't see his mother's stabbed and bludgeoned body sprawled out on the floor. In the kitchen was the body of his dead father, killed by a self-inflicted gunshot wound.

INTERVIEWING GOD

I.Y. WADE

Interviewing God

REV 19: 11-13

And I saw the heavens opened, And look! A white horse.

And the one seated upon it is called Faithful and True,

and judges and carries on war in righteousness.

Her eyes are a fiery flame, and upon Her head are many diadems.

She has a name written that no one knows but She Herself,

and She is arrayed with an outer garment sprinkled with blood,

and the name She is called is the Word of God.

Chapter I

John's cell phone rang. It was his Editor-in-Chief Mr. Conley.

"John get yourself down to Newspaper son. We've gotta' storm brewing the likes of which we haven't seen in years. I want you to take the lead on this one. You up for it?" Mr. Conley asked.

Of course, John was up for it. He'd been designated to minor copy-editing and fluff pieces for the last two years.

"Yes, sir. I'm on it. I'm just going to head home for a minute and make sure my aunt and uncle are okay. I'll head down to the office right after sir."

John tried to conceal his eagerness, but his editor knew he was anxious to prove himself. "Alright, don't let me down, son." Mr. Conley said hanging up the phone tersely.

John paid for his coffee and bran muffin. He left the waitress a hefty tip. He was on his way to becoming a full-fledged reporter.

As he walked into the parking lot, he could see the clouds turning ominously dark. The weatherman had reported that residents should prepare them-selves for the coming storm, but the way his editor sounded on the phone, this could be the storm that made his career. John started his truck and turned his radio to KFRM 550 AM.

"Good morning, Clay Center and all of the sur-rounding counties. This is Bob "The Z man" Zedekas coming to you live from the weather station at 550 AM; here to give you an update on that tornado that's heading our way. As of now, the National Weather Service has updated that tornado from an F1 to an EF3. What that means to you folks out there listening is simply this. An Ef, or Enhanced Fujita, is the amount of major property damage this storm is likely to cause. With that said, I can't emphasize enough that you need to get your animals inside, tie down all of that patio furniture, board those windows up, and stay in-doors until this thing blows over. We may be in for a wild ride."

As John pulled up to his aunt and uncle's home, his Uncle Paul was gathering plywood from the storage shed.

"Johnny you're right on time. Give us a hand will ya'?"

His uncle was the polar opposite of the man his father had become. Uncle Paul was gentle and loving. John couldn't have asked for a better foster father.

"No problem old man," John said grabbing an end of the plywood boards.

As he and his uncle went about the task of boarding up the windows, his Aunt Sarah came out the house and asked, "How are my two strong handymen making out?"

John nudged his Uncle Paul in the side and said, "He's killin' me, Aunt Sarah."

She responded, "Well ya'll two hurry up dinner is on the table."

His Uncle Paul replied, "We'll be right there."

As they boarded up the last window, the winds began to pick up. They went inside and ate what might be the last hot meal for quite some time.

John watched his aunt as she fixed their plates. Her face reminded him of his mother. While older, and her blonde hair now had slivers of gray, she looked much younger than most women her age. She would often say that it was "God's grace" that kept her young. As they sat and made small talk John suddenly remembered that he should have been down to the newspaper headquarters about an hour ago.

"Jesus Christ look at the time. I have to get outta' here."

His uncle reprimanded him, "Johnny you know we don't take the name of the Lord in vain in this house young man."

John apologized to his Uncle Paul. In no way did he mean to be disrespectful to his uncle who happened to be the pastor of the local church. But if there was ever a point that John and his uncle would never see eye to eye on, it was religion. John had given up on God long ago. He couldn't bring himself to worship a God that would let his mother be brutally murdered.

Now, as much as they butted heads about religion, the thing they both stood firmly against was the use of drugs. John, his aunt, and his uncle had watched drugs destroy both his family and community. As a youth, he swore to himself that he would never use illicit drugs of any sort. As John was about to leave the warning sirens began to go off.

"Crap!" John thought to himself.

His uncle put his hand on his shoulder. "I don't think you'll be going anywhere anytime soon Johnny."

"I guess you're right, Uncle Paul."

His aunt chimed in, "Yes John, he is right. You're coming down to the storm cellar with us."

His uncle grabbed the contingency bag that he kept packed in cases of emergencies. It had batteries, two flashlights, a few M.R.E's (meals ready to eat), and an MXT100 two-way radio. His Aunt Sarah brought along some blankets for what could be a long night.

"John, grab a case of water out of the pantry honey," his aunt said heading towards the door.

Outside the wind was howling. The three of them could barely stand as they made their way along the side of the house to the storm cellar. His uncle sat the duffel bag down as he fumbled searching for the keys. Paul inserted the key into the lock and pulled on the latch of the door. As he did a gust of wind snatched it open breaking his wrist. John and his aunt heard the loud crack as his uncle let go of the cellar door wincing and grabbing his arm in excruciating pain.

His Aunt Sarah helped her husband down the stairs while John picked up the duffel bag and the blankets off of the ground. He tossed the supplies into the cellar. With the case of water under one arm, he closed the cellar doors behind the three of them. His aunt rummaged through the duffel bag looking for a flashlight. Finding it, she searched around in the dark shining the light overhead until she spotted the string hanging from the light fixture. She pulled it illuminating the pitch black room. When she did, she and John could see the seriousness of his uncle's injury.

"Oh my goodness!" his aunt exclaimed when she saw the bone protruding through the skin of his uncle's lower forearm.

"We have to get him to a hospital, Aunt Sarah, his break looks bad," John said taking off his belt to make a tourniquet for his uncle's arm.

"No. We'll do no such thing, Johnny. It's too dangerous to drive in this weather. Sarah where's the medical kit?" his uncle asked.

She began searching around on the shelves in the cellar for the bag containing the medical supplies with no luck.

"We must have left it in the pantry closet, Paul, I'm sorry," she said visibly upset.

"It's not your fault dear. Johnny, I need you to go to the house and get the bag son. Can you do it?" he asked holding his wrist, grimacing.

"I'll be right back," John said climbing up the stairs.

He struggled against the force of the wind to push the door open. The sky was almost as dark as night now. He braced himself against the side of the house fighting the violent wind gust. John struggled to make it back to the porch. It was as if the wind was alive. When he opened the door to enter the house, it ripped the door off the hinges. The wind was now inside tossing furniture and ceramic pieces that had been neatly displayed about like an angry thief looking for hidden valuables. John dropped to his knees and crawled to the kitchen. To the left of him was the pantry. He pried the door open and saw the medical kit sitting on the bottom shelf. He held on dragging it as he crawled back outside onto the porch. He got up to run.

The gargantuan tree that stood yards away from the house began to creak giving way to the force of nature that had nurtured it for over a hundred years. As John reached the cellar, the last sound he would hear would be the loud snap of an eight-foot branch falling and hitting him in the head. He fell face first losing consciousness.

When John came to, he found himself standing in front of a river that was simultaneously fear-inspiring and regal. He thought himself to be dreaming or concussed, which would explain the slight ringing in his ears. But once the ringing subsided, he heard the sound of chanting. Chanting that was coming from the other side of the river just beyond the bank. Although he couldn't make out what was being said, he could hear that it was in perfect unison.

Chapter II

Just beyond the river, onto the riverbank, stepped a man in a pristine white robe. He walked over, or more precisely, on top of the water and took John by the hand.

"Hello John, I am Simeon Peter. I am here to escort you to the house of our Father."

John was startled. His thoughts went from believing he was dreaming to, "I must be dead!" But he had no recollection of being killed. "So how could that be?" he wondered.

St. Peter answered his thoughts. *"No one knows the moment when death comes for them brother. But no John, you are not dead. You have merely been summoned by our Father."*

John couldn't believe his ears. "How do you know my name? And how do you know what I'm thinking?" John asked.

"In Heaven, there are no secreted thoughts, only truths." St. Peter replied.

John laughed nervously.

"There must be some mistake. I don't believe in Heaven- or God," he said to St. Peter while marveling at the beauty that he was surrounded by.

Off in the distance, John saw babies with multi-colored wings of purple, blue, yellow, orange, and every other color of the rainbow and the color spectrum alike. He had mixed emotions about seeing these beautiful angelic cherubs because somehow he knew that they had to have died to receive such striking wings.

St. Peter responded, *"There is no need to feel sadness for these infants brother. When they perished, they felt no pain. Only the warm embrace of our Father's eternal light. If there is to be any grief, it is only because so many of these infants were aborted before they were able to serve the purpose for which God breathes life into them."*

The two came upon a glorious palace that far eclipsed the beauty of all of the things that John had witnessed thus far.

"This is where I leave you. Another will take you to meet our Father."

John felt uncomfortable the way St. Peter kept referring to God as "Our Father." God was no father of his. "His father" was a sadistic son of a... before he finished that thought, the doors to the magnificent dwelling opened, revealing a grand foyer filled with the religiously inspired works of da Vinci, Michelangelo, and all of man's monumental works of art, music and an opus of great literary works that venerated Almighty God.

Past the foyer, he saw a great room. In the middle of this room sat eleven thrones. The throne in the center was impressively large. It looked to be made of silver, white gold or perhaps platinum, and it appeared to glow. It was encrusted with every precious stone known to man. The throne on the right while not as stately as the first, was just as extraordinarily bejeweled. Followed by four less inspired thrones, but just as outstanding by anyone's standards. The thrones on the left of the center throne were the same as the four lesser thrones. That is except for the one furthest from the one in the center. This one appeared to be made of lead. Also as conspicuous, was that it was facing the rear of the great room. John walked toward the arrangement of thrones to touch them. As he did, an angel appeared from a room adjoining the foyer. She stood nearly nine feet tall.

"Hello, John, I am Sandalphina. I will be your counselor while you are here in Heaven."

She was beautiful. Her white wings extended down to just above her ankles. In contrast, her complexion was as black as coal. John stood there speechless in disbelief. Even with all that he had witnessed up to this point, his mind wrestled with the thought that he could have been wrong about God's existence for all of these years. Sandalphina sensed his angst.

"John, do you remember the last time you believed? I was there with you in the closet that evening. I, as well as our Father. He heard your prayers that night. He has never stopped loving you."

John stood quietly. Fifteen years had passed since that night. Fifteen years of unanswered questions. Fifteen years of not only skepticism but fifteen years of hate. Hate towards a God that allows the good of the Earth to suffer while the wicked flourish. When he encountered God, He'd have some explaining to do!

"Come, brother. It is time that you met our Father."

They exited that room and entered another. This room was void of furniture, and it had no ceiling, but it was no less splendid. John looked up in amazement. There above him lied the universe. He could see our solar system and beyond. It was filled with an infinite number of stars and planets. Comets sped past leaving behind trails of dazzling lights. As John watched in wonder, the figure of a sinewy Black woman came into the room.

"John come to Me, My child."

Sandalphina immediately dropped to one knee.

John found his voice.

"You can't be God. God is an old man."

The Creator laughed, *"That is an image or countenance that your historians and theologians believed I should have or resemble. But I am all things."*

As God spoke, He momentarily took on the likeness of an Indian Shaman. He then began to transmute between forms effortlessly. First, the form of an elephant, then, that of a young Asian boy, followed by the shape of a tree, and a number of other semblances before finally taking on the physique of an elderly bearded White man.

"Is this what you expected?" God asked smiling.

Before John could answer, a statuesque woman entered the room.

"Husband stop toying with the boy, he is confused enough."

She turned and faced John.

"Hello child, I am Asherah, The mother of creation. But throughout man's history, I have been called the Word, as in, 'In the beginning, the Word was with God.' I am a third of the Holy Trinity, but you may address me as the Queen Mother or simply Mother if that is what you like."

She turned and spoke to Sandalphina, *"Come here, daughter."*

Asherah's beauty was incomparable. If one could conceive of God having a wife; this is what she must look like. Sandalphina's wings began to flutter with excitement. Much like that of a puppy wagging its tail, elated to greet its master. Sandalphina bent and kissed her mother's cheek.

God sat on the floor and crossed His legs. When He did, Asherah and Sandalphina did likewise. God motioned for John to be seated as well. Then God spoke.

"I know you have many questions, My son. Be patient; all will be revealed unto you when you are ready. Just know that it has always been My sincerest wishes that this day would be avoided, since the day that the laws were given to Moses. But woefully, man has increased in his waywardness, more now than ever. More than in the days before Noah."

John sat listening. Asherah was right, all of this was very confusing. Heaven, angels, God! And now God has a wife? It was mind-boggling.

"Excuse me, your Highness," John said sarcastically addressing God. "I have a question or two. First, St. Peter told me that I'm not dead, so what am I doing here? Second, I'd like to know what's happened to my Aunt Sarah and my Uncle Paul. Are they alright?"

God answered very much aware of his sarcasm.

"You, My son, like so many others, are a soul waiting for judgment. As for your aunt and uncle- no child, they are not yet dead."

The words "not yet dead" stung John's ears. He heard nothing else.

"What? What do you mean not yet dead?" he yelled.

God's wife stood.

God raised His hand. *"Asherah remain seated."*

This time when the Almighty spoke lightning flashed across the Heavens.

He and Asherah had many disagreements about His decision to give man free will. She reasoned that man wasn't prepared for such freedom. A liberty that He had given to only a few of the archangels. The freedom to question, to think independently, the freedom to choose. A freedom that God had not given to any other species of the Earth.

It was that autonomy to choose that had abetted in man's disobedience. God realized that His beloved masterpiece would time and time again select riches over piety. The flesh over spirituality. God was saddened. It was man whom He commanded His angels to serve. Man, which caused His most trusted archangel Lucifer to seek to overthrow His reign. The same seed of man who now addressed Him with insolence.

Asherah embraced Her Husband. She understood the irony of how many passages in the Bible attributed jealousy, anger, strength, and love to God, but neglects to mention the dismay He feels because of mankind's rebelliousness. But it was of no consequence. John didn't know it, but this was the beginning of the end. The beginning of Armageddon!

"Daughter, send in Uriel," God said gesturing for Sandalphina to rise.

He then answered John's question, *"My child, why do you worry about the death of your loved ones? If I stated to you that they would perish in thirty years, one a day after the other, would that quash your concerns? Or would you then ask which of the two would expire first? I have tried to instill in all of mankind a passion for life. A life that in the beginning spanned hundreds of years. It is only because of sin that man's existences is extinguished like that of a flame. Do you consider the mayfly? Whose life is but a mere day, but still, it goes about doing the purpose that I have set forth. Does man think of the giant tortoise that lives for two hundred years? Slowly moving to and fro, unburdened, knowing that I will provide for all of its needs? No! You think only of yourselves, your loved ones, and your deaths. Your medical doctors and scientist labor in vain to extend life when I alone know the time and day of one's passing. It comes to me that mankind, My most precious creation, is My most self-seeking creation! So again I say - no, your loved ones are not yet dead!"*

The angel Uriel arrived and took a knee.

"Father, you have summoned me?"

God placed his hand on Uriel's back. *"Yes, My son, it is time."*

There was a different air about Uriel. John couldn't put his finger on it, but Uriel didn't come across as warm as Sandalphina. Uriel spread his massive wings without speaking a word to John and engulfed him. John could hear the sound of wind rushing past his ears. When they came to a halt, Uriel unfurled his wings and John saw that they were aboard a Chinese fishing trawler.

All about fishermen were busy casting huge nets into the water while others were manning outriggers and frenetically lowering cages off the side of

17

the vessel. They were yelling at each other in Chinese and throwing chunks of bloody chum into the sea. John didn't understand what was being said, but what he saw needed no explanation. Lined along the deck, in large steel bins filled to the top, were shark fins.

Uriel turned to John and said, *"Look at the ruin mankind is capable of."*

John didn't reply, he simply turned and watched as the crew started to pull in the enormous nets. There were easily ten to fifteen sharks in the one, but the other contained a behemoth-sized fish. The men yelled, "Jìngshā! Jìngshā! (Whale shark! Whale shark!)." They threw chained hooks attached to pulleys into the sea to hoist the creature on board. The fishermen began to hack at it with machetes mercilessly. As they did this, John saw that there were dark, winged beings surrounding them. They seemed to be whispering in the fishermen's ears.

John wanted to know who, or what these beings were, but before he could speak, an angel exited the sea. His name was Ariel. He was the guardian of every species of animal that swam in the ocean, walked the Earth (with the exception of man), or flew in the air. He was noticeably smaller than Sandalphina and Uriel, but unquestionably no less striking.

"Brother," he said crying, *"Do you see what they do?"*

Still alive, its body dismembered and spewing blood from its mouth, the men turned their attention away from the whale shark. They were now cutting the fins off of the sharks from the first haul and throwing the bodies back into the water, leaving them to starve, drown, or be eaten by other predators.

Uriel looked at Ariel and said, *"It is time we took leave brother."*

Suddenly, clouds formed and the sea began to churn. Thunder, lightning and blinding rain soon followed. Uriel took John by the arm and gruffly pulled him close. As they left, John could see the ship's crew frantically throwing lifeboats into the water and abandoning ship as the sea swallowed the vessel. Their efforts would be pointless. Their lives would not be spared.

When they arrived back in Heaven John would have more questions for God. He hoped that he would see Sandalphina. Besides God, no one else seemed to care for him. Uriel was indifferent, if not cold towards him, and Asherah, or "Mother," was ready to take his head off when he had raised his voice to God. Uriel left John outside of the palace. He heard the chanting again. This time it was louder. He walked in the direction it was coming from. It sounded like thousands. As he drew near, he made out what they were chanting.

"Death, destruction, the end of man!"

In front of what looked like an army in waiting, was a helmeted man on a white horse. He was riding up and down their ranks waving a flaming sword. As he did the chanting grew louder still.

"Death, destruction, the end of man!"

John walked closer. What he saw filled him with a fear he hadn't felt since he was a child. It was the savior of the world, "Jesus Christ" himself. John turned and went into the palace.

Inside God was sitting on His throne, but He was not alone. He was accompanied by Asherah and on each throne sat an angel. That is except for two. The one to His immediate right, and the one made of lead which was still facing the rear of the room. He was speaking to the angels who were attentively listening.

John approached them. This time when he addressed God, he spoke with a bit more reverence. "God, or Father, with all due respect," he said holding out his hands. "I, I'd like to know what's going on? I mean right before the boat sank, not only did an angel come up out of the friggin' sea..." He sheepishly looked at God, and the angels and said, "I didn't curse." He continued on, "I see these hideous winged beings lingering around the fishermen, whispering to them like they were egging them on. All the while they looked like, I don't know, like they were prancing as the ship's crew mutilated those sharks. Seriously-what were those grotesque looking things?" he asked in earnest.

God stood up.

"Those My son, are My children, your brothers," He answered.

John was alarmed. "How could that be?" he asked himself. "Everything in Heaven is beautiful beyond belief," he thought. His mind was racing.

God answered as if on cue, *"John there are many angels, My son. There are the archangels whom I created from light. They dwell in the Heavens as My faithful soldiers carrying out My commands without delay. To them, I have given sovereignty over all other angels. They are fourth in Heaven's hierarchy."*

John raised his hand as if he were in class and asked God a question, "If the archangels are fourth, then who's second and third?"(Even with his doubt, John knew that God would always be the head.)

God laughed, *"My child it goes without saying. It would be quite apparent to anyone that is anyone who has a wife. Asherah is My second in command. She would have it no other way,"* God said lightheartedly.

"There are the half-angels who walk the Earth amongst men. They are conceived by angels and man. They are the ones who have advanced your sciences and medicines. Some have become your leaders, using their innate gifts for the betterment of mankind, although not all are benevolent," God said frowning. *"Then there are those angels that you witnessed when you first crossed the holy waters. They are the young. Children who have been murdered, perished accidentally, or those who have died of natural causes. They and all of the unborn are granted divine passage, for they are all innocent in My eyes."*

John hung on God's every word as He spoke. He began to understand how people who believed in God could become enraptured with Him. God, in a word, was mesmerizing!

"Then there are those who have become angels through self-sacrifice. They have given their lives to save another. They are the ones whom men call heroes. In them, I take special delight. But, alas, in answer to your query, the last of these angels are the 'fallen.' They are the ones who chose to follow the deceiver, the accuser of men. The

one whom I placed above all other archangels. He was My third in command. Dispatched because of his disobedience."

God paused, and then said his name. A name that strikes dread into the hearts of man.

"Lucifer the bearer of light. Because these angels chose to side with him and sought to overthrow My reign, I condemned them to walk the Earth and dwell in Hell as vile-looking creatures, repugnant to man, and all in Heaven alike. For they are no longer angels, but demons! That is why they were whispering to the men on the fishing vessel. They want mankind to join them in Hell before their judgment is rendered. They willfully incite man to do evil. For that is what they do. They provoke and possess. While My Faithful are ever present to encourage and inspire humanity to choose a path of righteousness. For that is what I have given them to do. But know this child of man," God said sternly, pointing His finger at John, "The Earth is inhabited by men who are half-demons as well. So beware-wherever mankind inhabits the Earth, there are demons and half-demons. But you may take comfort in knowing that wherever there are demons, there are angels and half-angels. Man has only to decide whom he will listen to."

With that, God clapped His hands together. *"Enough! It is Saturday the Sabbath. It is time that we ready the festivities."*

The angels came off of their thrones to God's side.

"John this is Michael. My most trusted general. He is the foremost advocate for mankind and My fiercest warrior."

God then named the archangels in succession with their attributes. *"This is Uriel whom you have already been acquainted with. He is man's guide in the last days."* God then introduced an angel who was not as beautiful as the rest of the archangels. He had a scar traversing from the left side of his forehead to the right side of his chin. *"John, this is Gabriel. He is the messenger. The first to alert me of Lucifer's betrayal. The first to be scarred in the battle between good and evil. And while he looks fearsome, fear him not, for he only bears good fruit."*

God approached another archangel and said, *"This is Raguel. He has charge over man's morality. A task that keeps him very busy."* God chuckled and pointed to the next angel in the assemblage. *"Ramiel is the nurturer of man's hope and faith. He is tireless and ever opti-*

mistic." He then turned to Sandalphina. *"You have already become acquainted with My daughter. She is the one who hears all of man's prayers, and petitions on his behalf as well. And this one, he is the most sensitive of all of My cherished ones,"* God said placing his hand on the head of the youngest looking archangel in the throne room. *"He is Ariel. His duties are to watch over the species of the Earth. Sadly those species numbers are becoming less as man destroys their habitats or hunts them into extinction."*

God extended His hand in John's direction and said, *"Everyone this is John."*

The Angels did something John wasn't expecting. They all kneeled in front of him, heads bowed.

God explained, *"You see John, how My faithful willingly serve man! But I sense you detect that Uriel has some misgivings about you, and yes, you are correct in that assumption. It is because all of Heaven knows you believe yourself to be an atheist."*

The word atheist echoed in John's ears. He suddenly felt ashamed. All of his life his aunt and uncle had tried to convert him, but they understood his resistance. They believed when the time was right he would come to God of his own accord. John wanted to explain himself to God and the angels, but God stopped him.

"There is no need. I know, My child. There is nothing that you think, say, or do that I am not aware of." God then smiled and said, *"I know your heart. That is why I have brought you here. Now again I say, enough. It is the Sabbath."*

They exited the palace and went out into Heaven. The sound of chanting was absent, and in its place was the sound of Beethoven playing the piano and Louis Armstrong on the trumpet as angels strummed along on harps made of gold. All of Heaven sang hymns glorifying God's grandeur. There was food and wine set out on large tables. Everywhere you looked the young were playing; flying about chasing one another as though playing tag. Suddenly the throngs parted. Then John saw him. Jesus the Christ! Still at his side was the sword that He had swung zealously when rallying the angels that stood in formation. He walked up to God and kissed his hand.

"Father, we await your word."

The sight of Jesus with a sword took John aback. This was not the Christ that his mother had taught him about as a boy. Surely not the Christ that his uncle preached about? To the best of his recollection, the Christ he heard about was a teacher, a carpenter, and pacifist. You know, "The Lamb of God!" But the sword was trivial compared to his appearance. Jesus had brown skin and a head full of curly black hair. He wasn't the blonde, blue-eyed Jesus that he saw in the stained glass windows in the churches. Not by a longshot. This Jesus, God's Jesus was Black!

"John, this is My third in command. My spirit incarnate. In all of Heaven, there is only one Christ, one Lord, one Demi-God."

God beamed as He introduced His son. Jesus nodded His head in acknowledgment.

"Father, the first of the two horsemen, have been busy on the Earth." He stood holding His helmet in hand. *"There is pestilence and war in every corner of the world. Famine and death await your command as do your legions,"* Jesus said, his demeanor unwavering.

John wondered what his aunt and uncle would think of this Jesus. His complexion like that of an Ethiopian. "Not that they would have a problem with that," he thought to himself. But what would certainly cause them some consternation, would be seeing their "Prince of Peace" draped in full body armor, preparing to lead an army. John couldn't help noticing that Jesus seemed unconcerned with the celebration going on around Him. He got the same vibe from Jesus that he had gotten from Uriel, cold and apathetic. God whispered something to Jesus who then turned and left.

"Excuse me, Father," John said.

Calling God, Father was becoming easier for him.

"What's up with Jesus?" he asked. "I mean I get it. Everyone in Heaven knows that I'm an atheist. So I understand some resentment on their part, but I thought the one thing Jesus is supposed to be big on is forgiveness. Is there something I'm not getting?"

God sat down at the head of the great table and said, *"There will be time enough for your questions tomorrow. Please sit child; it is the Sabbath."*

Chapter III

Early the next morning John awoke to the sight of the sun shining brightly. He stood up, stretched, yawned, and rubbed his full belly. The food the night before was terrific. As was the wine.

"God really knows how to party," he mumbled.

"Yes, He does," he heard a familiar voice say.

John looked up. It was Sandalphina.

"Good morning brother. Did you sleep well?"

John yawned again. "Like an angel," he said squinting.

The sun seemed as though it was close enough to touch.

"But something has been bothering me," he said. "I have the chance to do what any man, or woman, has to literally give their lives to do, which is ask God any and everything. But every minute I spend here, the questions become more of an enigma than before. By no means am I clueless, I get it. If there's one place an atheist should feel out of place- it's Heaven. So what? God brought me here so Jesus, and everyone else could play dump on the heathen?"

He walked over to a fountain and splashed water on his face.

"John, it is not what you think. The reason our Father has summoned you here is because you are an atheist. Uriel and our Lord would be callous to any man. Not you alone."

"But why?" John asked. "What has man done that Christ and the angels in Heaven have such disdain for us?"

Sandalphina bowed her head and answered John.

"Nowhere on the Earth is there righteousness. You die from cancer while the peddlers of tobacco grow wealthy. The manufacturers of your weapons look away while your children are murdered in the streets of your nations. Your children are taught to pledge allegiance to your country's flag, while your lawmakers lobby to remove prayer from your schools," Sandalphina briefly stopped before going on, *"There is more mercy for an unbeliever than for those who believe and obey man's laws, but keep not the laws of God! That is why our Father has instructed me to give you counsel. I am tasked with helping you find that which you seek. The reason you are here,"* she said beckoning for John to accompany her.

He followed her asking where they were going.

"Uriel and Michael are to take you to speak with the ruler of the Earth," Sandalphina replied rather succinctly.

"Here we go again," John said. "More riddles."

This time Sandalphina gave him no response. They entered the Throne room and saw God joined by the archangels as well as Christ and Asherah.

"John, good morning child!" God exclaimed jubilantly. *"Today you have much to see before meeting him that has dominion over man. You will be traveling with My wife this day. Fear not child you will be well taken care of."* God looked at Asherah and said, *"Please take him, My love."*

Asherah stood up. *"Of course, Husband,"* She answered and immediately walked to John and embraced him.

When She held him, there was a discernable difference. While it was true that when Sandalphina engulfed him in her wings, it had indeed felt warm. In contrast to when Uriel snatched him like the business end of a doorknob, Asherah's touch was like that of a loving mother.

"Come child," She said. As the light sped by, Asherah spoke to him. *"I alone have the power to bend the constraints of time. There is none in Heaven who is more powerful than I. Not even God,"* She stated. Sensing the gravity of her words She sought to simplify things for John. *"Do you play chess child?"* She asked.

John nodded his head yes.

"Well, then you understand. You see although every piece on the board is in capitulation to the king, there is no piece more powerful than the queen. She moves about freely with one purpose- to protect her king."

The two of them came to a stop. When they did, John was up to his neck in water and debris.

"What is this place?" he asked splashing around, trying to keep afloat.

"This My child is called the Great Pacific Garbage Patch. An Island of refuse. Quite an ironic title wouldn't you agree? Since there is nothing great about this filth."

There were plastic bottles, toys, ocean buoys, and other non-degradable materials forming a large mass as far as the eye could see. In the midst of all of the floating trash, was an emaciated seal pup with a plastic container on its snout clinging to life. Asherah walked atop the water over to the young seal and knelt. She gently removed the bottle from the animal's mouth and rubbed her hand across the entire length of its body. When She did, it became revivified. The seal pup let out a guttural bark as it dove deep beneath the depth of the trash. Asherah took John's hand and lifted him fifty feet into the air. What he saw was disturbing. For miles, as far as the eye could see and beyond, was debris. While John was appalled, he held onto the fact that he wasn't personally responsible for the destruction.

"What can I do?" John asked. "My family and I recycle. What more is there?"

Asherah made no comment. She pulled John in, and they were off. When they came to a halt, it was dark out, but John could tell they were in a small city. John wasn't sure which city, but he noticed that the cars on the street were older model vehicles.

"We are in Bridgeport Connecticut in the year 1968."

As Asherah spoke, John noticed two men walking holding hands. A car pulled up slowly behind them and out jumped four young men. They began to taunt the men.

"Hey, you. Yeah, you two queers!" One of the men yelled.

Then John saw them. Demons! They were in the midst of the men as they followed the couple who were now walking faster. One of the instigators ran up behind the men and grabbed one of them by the arm. He spun him around and hit him across the head with a billy club. As he fell to the ground, the other three assailants began attacking his partner. It was brutal. The men were screaming for help. John looked to Asherah to intervene.

She looked back at him and said, *"Watch child."*

John could see neighbors coming to their windows and peeking out. Somewhere out of a window, a woman hollered, "Leave those men alone, or I'm calling the police."

John could see an angel beside her in the window frantically coaxing her. But the men kept up the attack as though they were possessed. What they did next was incomprehensible. While one sat on the chest of one of the men and pinned his arms down, two others pulled his pants down to his ankles and held his legs spread eagle. The fourth man removed a pair of garden shears from inside his college varsity jacket. He knelt down, as he did the man's lover came to, but it was too late. A demon had his hands on top of the young man's hands with the shears guiding him as he castrated the man.

"Whatcha' gone do with no pecker Nancy boy?" he asked mockingly, his hands covered in blood.

The man's lover screamed for a God who was said to have despised him, "No! Oh my God, no!"

The men left the mortally wounded man on the ground, blood spewing everywhere, and turned their attention to his partner. As they approached him, Asherah shrieked, *"Begone!"*

34

When She did the demons froze in their tracks.

"It is the Queen Mother! Run! Our work is done here, brothers. Let us go."

They slunk off into the night.

Lightning cracked in the night's sky. As it did the woman who was in the window came downstairs with a German Shepherd that was growling and barking menacingly. When they saw the woman and the dog the men stood up.

"Why don't you mind your business you old hag?"

She let out the leash a little and pulled a gun out of her bathrobe.

"This is my business," she said. In the background, the sound of police sirens was drawing near. The men stopped and ran to their vehicle.

"Forget her," one of them yelled.

It began to rain as the man lay dying in his partner's arms. The woman was bent down beside the men attempting to console them both. John saw the angel that had been in the window with the woman reach down and touch the hand of the injured man. When he did the man's body went limp. His soul left his body and joined the angel on the journey toward

Heaven. The police arrived soon after with an ambulance close behind.

"You have seen ample for now child, come."

This time as they traveled Asherah was silent.

They arrived back in the Throne Room.

"What have you learned today child?" God asked.

"I learned what I knew all along. Man is filthy and violent," he said.

God understood John's anger, so He answered him accordingly, in the gentle tone of a parent admonishing a young child.

"No, son," God said, *"That was not the lesson. What you saw today was the danger of the self- righteous standing idle in judgment while the wicked run amok. Apathy is an unwritten sin, but no less irredeemable."*

John interjected, "But there was a woman who came out to help."

"Yes, there was. But there were others; men, and women who heard the screams of the men and did nothing. Not because they were afraid, but because they knew of these men and their relationship, and they cared not about their fate."

John pondered before replying, "If I'm not mistaken but in the bible, isn't homosexuality a sin?"

God answered John with a parable, *"If a man*

36

has two daughters, the one who is married is an adulterer, and the other who is without a husband is promiscuous in the land, who does the father love or scorn more?" Before John could answer God spoke again, "Since the law was given to Moses, man has sought to find ways to set himself apart from his brother. Choosing which sin they think I should consider the most detestable. Eat that which I say is forbidden, take My name in vain, kill the unborn, and disregard the Sabbath. But what man reasons I should find the greatest transgression - is man loving man!"

John stood quietly.

"Daughter take him to the garden."

Sandalphina took John by the hand and walked him into a garden. Birds were singing in the trees, animals of every species freely walked the grounds. In the center of the garden was a beautiful apple orchard. Midpoint of that was a beautiful tree with a strange fruit hanging from its branches. A fruit that John had never seen before.

When Sandalphina observed John looking at it, she quickly told him, "Our Father has said to all that are in Heaven that we may eat all that we wish, but we must not eat from that tree. The tree of knowledge of good and evil."

He shrugged his shoulders. His interest had shifted to the chanting that had begun outside the garden again.

"Death, destruction, the end of man."

Sandalphina sat on the grass wet with dew.

"Please brother, come sit with me."

She picked a flower and gave it to John. He inhaled the scent of it.

"Brother you are being shown these things because the time will come when you will have to decide. You must know that our Father does nothing that is not for our betterment. When a loved one becomes sick or dies, or when one experiences loss, there is a lesson to be learned in all of these things." She placed her hand under John's chin. *"Consider the words of the disciple Matthew when he said, 'It rains on the righteous and the unrighteous alike.'"* She continued, *"But it is how we view the rain that determines our place in the kingdom. The unrighteous will question God, as to why? While the just will know and understand that the rain is a necessary part of life. They will simply say, God's will is done; glory be to God!"*

John fully grasped the narrative of the rain. He knew that it symbolized the trials and tribulations that people go through. The pain that seemed senseless was sometimes needed to teach a lesson, and other times are necessary to prepare one for what was to come. But still, he questioned what could've been the lesson in his mother being taken away from him at such a young age?

Sandalphina stood, *"In time you will know all that you need to know brother. But now you are going with Uriel and Michael. Stay close to them, and trust not your eyes or ears, only your heart."*

John stood up and asked, "Why? Where am I going?"

Sandalphina's answer was unexpected, *"To Hell brother."*

John's eyes opened wide.

"What do you mean to Hell?" he asked.

"You are going to meet him who has been given authority over mankind," she replied.

Uriel and Michael entered the garden in military regalia. They encircled John with their wings and began to pray, *"O how you have fallen from Heaven, you shining one, son of the dawn! How you have been cut down to the Earth, down to Sheol, the remotest parts of the pit."*

Their journey was brief, and when the three of them came to a halt, Uriel said, *"We are here."*

John surveyed his surroundings. Hell wasn't at all what he assumed it would be. You know dark, the smell of sulfur burning, demons standing over the wretched with tridents keeping them at bay; writhing

39

in a burning lake of fire. It was nothing like that at all. In fact, Hell seemed as though it was one big party. Skyscrapers with neon lights were everywhere, flashing the name of this club, that bar. It looked like a scene from a Hollywood movie depicting the Las Vegas strip.

In a blatant juxtaposition to Heaven, noticeably absent was someone to greet them at the gates of Hell. Which was also not gated at all. Hell was wide open just as Heaven was. The streets were flooded with crowds of people, but unlike Heaven, no one was scurrying about. Everyone was laid back and carefree. That is everyone except Michael and Uriel, who had drawn their swords which burst into flames as they unsheathed them.

"Keep watch brother," Michael said to Uriel.

As they traveled, a woman came out of a nightclub. She had pale skin which was covered in tattoos and piercing eyes that were as green as emeralds.

"Mikey, how are you love? Long time no see. And will you look at you Uriel, all big and strong! I just love the muscles," she said grabbing one of Uriel's biceps. She played with her long black hair while eyeing John.

"And who is this human?" she asked reaching out to touch John's face.

40

Michael placed his sword at her neck. *"Go away from us, Jezebel. We have no dealings with you harlot. We are here to see your master."*

Jezebel stepped back. *"Well, why didn't you say so? No need to be nasty,"* she said motioning for them to follow her.

As they walked, John saw people drinking and smoking. Men and women were scantily clad gyrating on the dance floor to lust-filled lyrics driven by seductive beats.

"Hell is pretty bad ass!" he said to his companions before he hesitated momentarily. "Nope. No thunder," he smiled. "I could get used to this."

As they traveled on, he saw soldiers in a variety of uniforms from different time periods and regions. Soldiers in Roman garb drank from gold chalices. Others soldiers with SS insignias on their collars laughed and sang a song in German as they kicked their legs as though they were in a chorus line. "Wir sind das Heer vom Hakenkruez, Hebt hoch die roten Fahnen! Der deustchen Arbeit wollen wir, Den Weg zur Freiheit bahnen!"

John had no idea what the words meant that they sang, but they were clearly loud and off-key.

There were soldiers dressed in the blue and gray uniforms of the North and South of the Civil War. To him, it was understandable why the soldiers of the South might be in Hell because they fought on the wrong side of slavery, but he was puzzled about the soldiers of the North. "Why would they be in Hell?" he thought. But they were but a minuscule demographic in what was a sea of people.

What John didn't see were children. In such a diverse crowd there was not one child.

"God must really love kids," he said.

They finally came to a stop. In front of them was an opulent mansion that was twice the size of God's palatial estate. Michael stood in front of John while Uriel covered the rear. There weren't any doors on the residence and inside the three observed orgies involving numbers too many to count. Michael and Uriel were unfazed by the indecency, but John became aroused and embarrassed all at once.

An alluring voice called out, **"Hello, brothers. What brings you to my humble abode?"** The one asking was quite, well... beautiful. He wore a silk bathrobe and had slippers on his feet. He was surrounded by naked men and women who were titillating, to say the least.

Michael spoke, *"Greetings Lucifer,"* he said putting his blade away. Uriel lowered his sword but kept it at the ready. *"Father has instructed us that we show the man-child the consequences of sins, great and small,"* Michael said.

John noticed men on the other side of the room. He strained to get a better look. Satan saw him looking and called for the men to come nearer. Out of the shadows emerged Adolf Hitler.

"Of course," John thought.

But who he didn't expect to see hobnobbing was a scientist in a lab coat.

"Ah, Robert come here, meet our guest. John, right?" Satan asked. "John this is Dr. J. Robert Oppenheimer. The distinguished Dr. Oppenheimer of the Manhattan Project." John was lost.

Like many from his generation, he had never heard of the Manhattan Project. The single most important military initiative of the twentieth century, the making of the atomic bomb! He was joined by Joseph Stalin, Idi Amin, George Washington, Pol Pot, Christopher Columbus and a number of men and women dressed in religious attire.

"This John is my inner sanctum!" Satan exclaimed exuberantly.

Michael reprimanded him, *"Show him, brother. Show him the wages for disobeying our father. The recompense of sin, or will you try to deceive him as you have all of his siblings?"*

Lucifer placed his hand on his chest. John saw that his fingernails were impeccably manicured. "Moi?" he asked mockingly. "How have I deceived man? I have always been forthwith in telling man that all he desires shall be laid at his feet if only he would choose to take control of his destiny. Why if it weren't for me man would still be walking around unclothed in some garden, no sciences, no technology, no television, and let's not forget the internet. Ohhh how I love the internet. With the pressing of a few keys, you can view debauchery, decapitations, dismemberment, child pornography, bestiality and anything else one's blackheart desires. I couldn't imagine life without the internet? But really, let's be frank, all that man is-is because of me!" he said flopping back down on his marble throne. "Still, with all of my urging, and dare I say prayers, man's evil has surpassed my wildest dreams, there is nothing that man will not do for riches. Pride, lust, envy, gluttony, sloth, and wrath, which is my second favorite of the seven deadly sins, pales in comparison to greed!"

As Lucifer spoke, John gazed and saw Pablo Escobar lingering in the shadows talking with Caligula, and a group of young men with a variety of colored handkerchiefs covering their faces. John assumed they were gangbangers.

"Man will do anything for money, power, and for reasons that even I don't understand," Satan chuckled. "For example, those fellows goose stepping ever so jubilantly as you walked in are some of Hitler's top aides. Hold on. Let me set the stage." With a wave of his hand, a spotlight appeared and followed him as he pranced around like a diva. "Ladies and gentleman, put your hands together for another exciting episode of *How the hell did I get here!* Let's see first up, one of the main architects of the Holocaust who oversaw the extermination of one million Polish Jews in Nazi extermination camps, most notably Treblinka, let's give a warm hades welcome for SS-Standartenführe…Odilo Globocnik!"

Off in the background john heard cheering and loud whistles.

"Coming second to the dais not to be outdone by his comrade, 'The Angel of Death,' although we down here like to say "The Demon of Death." It has a melodic ring to it if you know what I mean." Out stepped an unremarkable, if not average looking man with a smile on his face. "Josef Mengele! His inhumane medical experiments, and the delight he took in the misery of those interned at Auschwitz as he conducted those experiments sent chills down the spine of even the most callous amongst us.

Whew," Satan said pantomiming as if he were shivering.

He continued on rambling off a "Rogue's gallery" of some of the most revolting human beings to ever walk the Earth.

"Now, for you fellows out there who think the ladies aren't capable of being just as abhorrent as yourselves, I present Ilse Koch, 'The Bitch of Buchenwald.' She, my friends selected prisoners with tattoos that piqued her nefarious interest, had them killed and their tattooed skin removed to make lampshades to display in her home."

Ilse Koch curtsied and blew a kiss towards the Prince of Darkness.

"Joining her is Ms. Mary Ann Cotton, who killed three husbands, one lover, her mother, eleven of her children and her sister in law, whom she also held to be a close confidant" Lucifer put his hand up to the side of his cheek and said, "Sheesh, with friends like her who needs enemies?"

Although Satan made light of the heinousness of these acts, John was beginning to see him for what and who he was- pure evil!

"Last, but certainly not least, rounding up our hellish version of ladies night out, Mrs. Amelia Dyer, 'The Ogress of Reading.' She alone killed four hundred of those that are closest to our father's heart, his beloved infants," he declared with a hint of derision.

John was horrified. As he looked closer, he saw that the ambiance he first thought so enthralling, was repugnant. The festivities had stopped. The faces of the revelers were actually an assembly of murders, rapist, sadist, and deviants. John Wayne Gacy stood there in his clown costume conversing with Ted Bundy. Griselda Blanco was laughing and having drinks with Thug Behra, who admitted to strangling over one hundred and twenty–five men himself and presiding over the murders of up to nine hundred and thirty others. John overheard Ken Lay telling Vlad the Impaler and Mao Zedong how he couldn't wait to meet up with his ol' buddy Bernie Madoff. While Vlad the Impaler gushed whom he was waiting to meet was "La Bestia" the beast, Luis Garavito, one of the most prolific child killers in modern history.

John approached Michael and asked him; no, demanded that they go, saying he had heard and seen enough.

Somewhere in Michael's spirit he took pity on John and agreed that he had indeed seen enough.

"Wait!" Lucifer shouted, "Before you depart I have one more soul to present to you. While he has not killed millions, thousands, or even hundreds, he did kill himself and his wife while she was trying to protect their young son. But more than that, I think John will find a personal connection to him. So without further ado, I give you Mr. Kyle McKinneth."

"You're lying!" John screamed. "You're lying!" he repeated. "That's not my father!"

He yelled backing away. As he did Uriel ran towards Lucifer with his sword poised for battle. Just as quickly, Satan's minions stepped forward to protect their master. Uriel's blade lopped off an arm. As it fell to the floor, Satan rose to his feet.

"You have no power in my house!" Satan roared transforming into a monstrous creature.

In place of the once striking "Morning Star" stood a being with the head of a dragon with three eyes that gazed upon Michael, Uriel, and John, separate, but simultaneously. His skin which had an appearance like that of a swine was covered in boils that oozed an odorous black and foul discharge. Six-inch claws protruded from the beast's hands and feet. From the trunk of his body grew a tail that flung wildly back and forth. Flanking his back were tattered soot covered wings that beat furiously as he moved pushing his sycophants out of his path to get to the objects of his wrath.

The images of Hell began to change as well. All around him John now saw flaming pits filled with the bodies of the lost begging for mercy and deliverance. Michael held John close while swinging his sword removing Lucifer's flock's heads from their frames. As the two angels continued battling, they carved a path through the demonic hordes. Smoke left the bodies of their fiendish host leaving behind a pile of ash. Satan was livid.

"You want the human to know the truth?" he bellowed. "The truth is man needed no encouragement to defy our Father. It took little coaxing to get Eve to eat the forbidden fruit. She had grown weary of the mundane life that God had set aside for her and Adam in the Garden of Eden. She longed for more as all mankind did and does. I merely have to show man wealth, and given the opportunity, they will betray our Father time and time again. That is my truth brothers."

Satan held up his hand to his followers who halted in their tracks. Michael and Uriel were covered in their putrid blood.

"Has our father told the man-child the truth?" he asked as he took his former physique. The angels put away their flaming blades.

"What is he talking about?" John asked Michael.

"Oh, you don't know do you?" Satan asked. "You don't know that He is going to destroy the Earth. After allowing me to reign for a mere thousand years, He wants to destroy those of you who choose to follow me, or more importantly, not follow Him! Lucifer declared. Now, who's the narcissist?" he asked.

His tirade fell on deaf ears, Michael and Uriel had no empathy for their fallen brother.

Michael turned and said, *"Come Uriel."*

They again embraced and began to pray.

"Wait!" Satan exclaimed.

They stood and waited for Lucifer to speak.

"Before you go tell, tell our father I miss him," he said.

Michael nodded and began to pray the Prayer that would deliver the trio home. The same prayer that delivers billions daily. The same prayer John had prayed that evening his mother died.

"Our Father in Heaven, Hallowed be thy name. Your Kingdom come, Your will be done on Earth as it Heaven. Give us this day our daily bread. And forgive us our trespasses as we forgive those who trespass against us. And do not lead us into temptation, but deliver us from the evil one. For Yours is the kingdom and the power and the glory forever. Amen."

Chapter IV

When they arrived back in Heaven John made haste to the Throne room. He was approached by Sandalphina.

"Brother, wait!" she besought him.

But John would have none of it. He walked briskly past her into the Throne room where God sat holding court. Michael, Uriel, and Sandalphina came in behind him and kneeled.

"Father I tried to stop him," Sandalphina said flustered.

"It's okay daughter. I've been expecting him."

John walked towards God with his head held low.

"I'm sorry Father," he said.

All of the sardonicism had gone from his tone. Of all the horrid things that he had seen, the image that haunted him the most was that of his father, his "real" father in Hell.

"Father you told me that there were circumstances that granted souls instant entrance into Heaven; I'm curious how does one's soul enter into Hell?"

This time John dropped to one knee when he addressed God and said, "Father."

God looked down at the child who had denied Him for so many years and was now kneeling in reverence.

"Perhaps there is yet hope for man," God wondered to Himself. *"Well child, there are many actions that condemn one's soul without mercy,"* God spoke pensively. *"Murder is the foremost of these acts. But murder shall not be misconstrued with the taking of a life in defense of your own. Nor the putting to an end of an evil committed against those who are weak,"* he said. *"The torture or maiming of a man, woman, or animal shall not be forgiven. Those who commit these acts their soul shall be condemned to Sheol."*

God continued as John listened intently.

"The rape of a man, woman, or child shall not be forgiven. Any man or woman who molests or fornicates with children shall not be forgiven. Those who take life from the womb shall not be forgiven. The hoarding of riches while neglecting the poor shall not be forgiven. Clerics who use My name to amass riches shall not be forgiven. Any ruler that causes war against another nation to amass riches shall not be forgiven. Those who bear witness to evil and do not act shall not be forgiven. Any man that

52

bears false witness against his brother, and causes his brother to be murdered shall not be forgiven." God paused and said, *"And finally My son, any man or woman who abuses a child shall not be forgiven!"*

"So what happens to all the other souls who don't fit into those two categories that you've mentioned?" John asked. "Those who aren't murders, or self-serving, you know, the ones who go directly to Hell? And what of those people who weren't heroes, or children that enter into Heaven without judgment? What happens to those millions of souls?" John asked.

"No John, not millions. Billions. There are exactly 98 billion, 780 million, 643 thousand, 2 hundred and 12 souls that await the rapture in Purgatory. I know their numbers as well as the number of hairs on each of their heads. I know the year, the day, and the second they perished. For it is I who hath welcomed them into Heaven, banished them to Sheol, or sent them to Purgatory to be judged," God replied.

John recalled the first time he had heard the word Purgatory. He remembered as a teenager asking his uncle what would happen to someone if they died and hadn't believed in God. His uncle did his best to explain it in terms that a child might be able to understand. He told John that he supposed that those who didn't believe in God when they died went to a place called Purgatory.

John's next question naturally was, "What's Purgatory unc'?"

His uncle thought for a moment and then asked, "Are you planning on dying anytime soon Johnny?"

John keenly remembered the answer he gave his uncle. "No, Uncle Paul. It's just that I was thinking about my mom and dad. I know my mom believed in God, but I'm not so sure about my father."

His response took his uncle by surprise.

"Out of the mouth of babes," his uncle said to himself.

At that time it had been five years since he had come to live with his aunt and uncle. And although he had cried over the loss of his mother many times in those five years, his Uncle Paul had no recollection of him mentioning his father up til' that point.

"Well, Johnny, as far as I reckon, Purgatory is a place where the souls of those who die go and wait for God to decide if the good they've done outweighs the bad. And if it does, then they'll get to go to Heaven, son," he said rather matter- of- factly; hoping his answer would satisfy his nephew's inquisitiveness. But like any teenager, John had another question.

"And what if they haven't done enough good unc'?"

His uncle answered him pithily, "Well son; then they go to Hell."

At the age of fifteen while he wasn't familiar with Purgatory, who in the world didn't have an idea what Hell was? In the years that had passed since that day, he'd always believed that his mother was in Heaven, and perhaps, just maybe his father was in Purgatory. As a young man growing up, that was good enough for him. But now at twenty- five, standing face to face with the Creator, he hoped for a more in-depth explanation. The sound of Gods voice brought him back.

"Purgatory is where the cleansing of the soul takes place. It is where those who have been neither hot nor cold shall face the flames of purification. Those same flames that the Lamb of God and the angels of Heaven wield to strike down the evil that dwells in the Earth and the demons of Sheol alike, My child."

John listened as God explained.

"Each soul according to its sin, or its state of grace, that is, the passage thru the purgative, illuminative, and unitive way which will determine that souls time in the flames."

John was again unsure of what God was talking about.

"Crud, just as it was beginning to make sense," he said beneath his breath. "God may as well have been speaking gibberish," he thought to himself.

"No John, not gibberish, it's quite simple," God replied. *The Purgative way or the beginning is the awakening of the moral self and the abstaining from sin."*

And then it happened. God did something wondrous and rare that had only been recorded once in the bible. He reached out and touched John. The engineer of the universe placed a hand upon John's head. While it's true, in the Old Testament God had ordered the smiting of individuals and nations alike, but more often than not these acts were carried out by the archangels or the Word, Asherah. Not since the forming of Adam and Eve, had God laid hands on a human being. When He did, John heard the blaring screams of mothers during childbirth, fused with the sight of an exploding star, succeeded by the sound of volcanoes erupting and crashing waves. But all of these were drowned out by the reverberation of God's now amplified voice.

"It is the state when one first seeks righteousness. This is then followed by the "Illuminative way" which is the progression that is made on one's spiritual journey. This is the state where you quickly overcome the greater sins but are still tempted by the lesser sins. The sins that manifest themselves in the mind, such as lust, envy, and pride. While these three sins prevail in the thoughts; the fourth sin, that of sloth is born in the mind as well as the flesh. It is due to one's being remiss or idle. That is the neglecting to perform one's duties to God, family, and, or those you are in service to."

As God spoke to John, visions of Purgatory slowly appeared. There were spirits kneeling all about him.

They pleaded, *"El Shaddai hear our prayers. We beg of You O' omnipotent One, the immutable One. You the Great Jehovah, Allah, and Yahweh. The Alpha and the Omega. The Beneficent, the Merciful. Praise be to God, the Cherisher and Sustainer of the worlds; The Beneficent, The Merciful; master of the Day of Judgement. You do we worship, and Your aid do we seek. Show us the straight way. The way of those whom You have bestowed Your Grace, those whose portion is not wrath, and who do not go astray. Amin and Selah."*

God ignored their petitions and turned His back on the wretched souls imploring Him for mercy.

"These two states are followed by the "Unitive way" or the state of perfection. The truly devout must endeavor years to attain this stature, and still few have done so. Those who do, ascend to sainthood, as do those who are persecuted and die in My name and in the name of the Christ."

As God continued speaking John's attention drifted. While he heard God's words, his focus was on the faces of those pleading, no, groveling for God's forgiveness. It was disturbing to see. Almost as disturbing as his excursion into Hell. But that wasn't it. What commanded John's gaze was their eyes. Their eyes were gray and clouded over like that of someone suffering from cataracts. Their empty stares gave John an eerie feeling that made the hairs stand up on the back of his neck.

"Child, do not become distressed?" God said. *"These hypocrites you see here before you are blinded now as they were blinded on Earth. They represent the self-righteous of the world, Protestant, Christian, Judaist, Muslim, and Catholic. They have all tortured, maimed, murdered, and accused the innocent in the name of religion. And although I have spared them the hellfire, I have condemned*

58

them to the flames of Purgatory for an indefinite number of days so that those souls who observe their suffering do not haughtily assume that their works in the church assure immediate clemency."

To add to the anguish of the condemned, there was the image of Heaven on the horizon. An ever-present reminder of paradise lost. God removed his hand from John's head and returned to His throne. The images of Purgatory vanished as God went on speaking. John could hear the screams of the ambivalent. Those who had earnestly sought God, but could not escape the snares of sin.

"But they are not alone in their anguish," God stated. *"Many more are made to endure the flames that sear not the flesh, but the soul. Those who bear false witness. Those who are adulterers. Those who fornicate wantonly. Those who have proclaimed themselves men of God while simultaneously oppressing My daughters and those of another race or religion. As well as those who praise My name on the Sabbath while indulging in iniquity in all the days leading up to the Sabbath,"* he paused looking around at His counsel.

"Then there are those who do good in the Earth for accolades and rewards. They lust for monuments to be

erected in their honor, or their names inscribed on the walls of men for all to see. All of these acts do I disallow!"

God raised His voice emphasizing His contempt. John thought for a moment before he said anything.

"So if I'm to understand," he said, "Everyone who's died since the beginning of time is either in Heaven if they're granted favor, or have done something you deem worthy. In Hell, if they've murdered, tortured, maimed, raped or abused. Which is pretty cut and dry I think," he said with a bit of levity, more out of nervousness than disrespect. "Or Purgatory if they're in between. Not quite pious, but not quite immoral. Am I right?" he asked the Almighty believing he finally had a grasp on the inner workings of the celestial.

But when God answered, *"No, My child, you are not."* John wasn't at all fazed.

He was no longer surprised by God's responses. He began to realize that with every answer there came more questions. This time before John could inquire further, God clarified the statement.

"The exception to these canons are the spirits who walk the Earth. The souls that men call ghost. Some have died violently, and they will not rest until their killers have been punished. Others have died quickly and know not that

60

they have perished. Still, others do not wish to leave their loved ones behind. All of these have I granted liberty until the rapture. And again, God said solemnly, as it is with demons and angels, there is a portion of these spirits that are benevolent while others are yet malevolent. Though they were not murderers as to be condemned forthwith to Sheol, they were evil nonetheless." And then God added, *"That is why I have forbidden man to communicate with the dead!"*

This time when God finished speaking there would be no questions to ask, although John speculated to himself where someone like his mother fit into God's divine equation.

INTERVIEWING GOD

Chapter V

"John, how are you, My child?"

It was Asherah.

"I'm fine... Mother," he replied after hesitating.

It was strange, while John found it difficult to call God Father at the beginning of their meeting when addressing Asherah, the appellation Mother, rolled off his tongue. And while John didn't know it, that too was a part of the grand design. God understood the need to make John feel at ease, even if he didn't.

She took John by the hand and said, *"You have seen many things, but before it is done there are many more things that must be shown to you, My son."*

John could only imagine what was to come. As the two of them stood there talking, Jesus Christ approached them. He repeated to Asherah what he had said to God.

"Mother, the Horsemen are loosed upon the Earth. There is no place that has not been ravaged by disease, affected by war, or has not known famine and death," he said kissing her hand.

"Thank you, My beloved," She replied while taking John into her arms.

"Are you ready child?" She asked him.

John nodded yes.

"Then it is time."

As the light passed the two of them by, John remembered that though the archangels could traverse from location to location without incantations, prayer was necessary when they traveled to and from Hell, but as Asherah implied She needed no such prayers. She merely spoke, and it became. Her beauty was eclipsed only by her power. When their journey came to an end, there was no garbage patch or small suburban town. No, this time they were in what appeared to be a present-day hospital. Much like any twenty-first century American medical facility. That is, except for what John thought was the Spanish being spoken over the PA system.

Asherah corrected him, *"No John that is Portuguese you hear. We are in Brazil, My child."*

John looked over his right shoulder and saw a nursery. Inside there were infants aligned in incubators side by side, wall to wall. There were crying mothers in hospital gowns with their faces pressed up against the glass. Some were comforted by the fathers of their children. Asherah told John to take a closer look at the children in the nursery. What he saw troubled him immensely. The nursery was filled with babies born with abnormally small heads.

"The children you see here are suffering from microcephaly," She said. *"Although there are many causes for this condition, here in Brazil it is caused by a disease transmitted by mosquitos to expecting mothers. In times past it has been solely viral in primates, but God has seen fit that it should now vex mankind."*

John's mind raced. He was again conflicted about his feelings toward God. He questioned as he had done many times in the past, how could a God of love and mercy punish the innocent? Especially the very babies that he pronounces to love above all of his creations.

Asherah answered him as was to be expected, *"Here in Brazil child prostitution is widespread, as is the murder of thousands perpetrated by the offspring of this beautiful country. Murders fueled by their lust for wealth."* She wiped a tear from her eye. *"If they do not value what is certainly their most priceless possessions, their children, then the affliction of their progeny shall open their eyes."*

Her words rang true. What could be more precious than the life of a child? This time when She took

John by the hand, they were transported to the favelas of Brazil.

"Look around child. We are in Rio de Janeiro. Tell me what you see."

It was late in the evening, but the streets were teeming with activity. John saw young children, both boys and girls walking up to strangers. He heard them speaking as they approached the people walking by them on the dirt strewn streets. Some of them tugging at the untucked tee shirts of the men and grabbing the hands of the women as they walked by.

"Qualquer coisa por um dòlar Ms.? Farei qualquer coisa por um senhor dòlar?"

Although John didn't understand what they were saying, the tone of their voice coupled with their gestures was implicit.

"Por favor, senhor Estou com fome."

Asherah walked over to John and touched his ear. When She did this their words were instantaneously translated, much to his dismay.

"Anything for a dollar miss? I'll do anything for a dollar, sir? Please, sir, I'm hungry?" the children pled.

John pulled his head away from the Queen Mother. He was sickened at the sight of grown men, some of them who looked to be European or American, going into alleys with young children, some as young as nine years old.

A young kid came running fast from around the corner. He looked no older than thirteen or fourteen. As he passed Asherah and John, shots rang out. John instinctively ducked, but Asherah stood fast while the bullets passed harmlessly through her and into the fleeing teenager. He collapsed in front of John with blood trickling from his mouth as his body lay motionless. A gang of six young thugs ran up and stood over the dying boy, guns in hand, and fired a barrage of shots into him. Sending a message to anyone who had the audacity to sell drugs in their neighborhood. People in the street darted into doorways and shops to get out of the way of the delinquents that ran the favelas. Two angels appeared in the midst of the confusion and grappled with the young man's soul. John watched in shock as the teen's spirit fought and cried in agony.

"What's happening Mother? Why is the boy's spirit fighting, doesn't he want to go to Heaven?" he asked bewildered.

"His soul knows that it is being taken to Purgatory child," She said stoically. *"Sadly, he is neither righteous nor*

evil, but misguided, and his soul must be purified in the flames."

With that said, She began to recite an ominous prayer, *"I am Asherah the Word. And by the power invested me from the Almighty God, the One who is and who was and who is coming; Look! I am about to throw her into a sickbed, and those committing adultery with her into great tribulation. And her children will I kill with a deadly plague."*

The sky turned dark, and the air was filled with the sound of buzzing. As it got closer, John saw millions upon millions of mosquitoes. He and Asherah watched as they besieged the hapless citizens and tourist of Brazil.

Asherah looked to the sky and shouted, *"Pestilence, My son, come. Let nowhere in the Earth be spared the scourge of your touch."*

The swarm of mosquitoes parted, and John saw an angel on a white horse galloping through the clouds past the statue of "Christ the Redeemer" with a crown on his head and armed with a bow.

"As you wish Mother. I will dispose of a third of man. They will beg to come into the fold of My Father's house."

He removed four golden arrows from his quiver and shot three of the four into three corners of the Earth. One toward the west, one to the east, one to the north, and the last he shot into the soil of South America. When he did the swarm diverged into four hordes. One quarter following a golden arrow in its own direction.

Asherah looked to Heaven and said, *"It has begun."*

She took John by the arm, and they were off. When they reached their next destination, John surveyed his surroundings and realized they were in a lab.

"Where are we?" John asked still looking around.

"We are where man will attempt in vain to prevent the onslaught that is to be," Asherah answered. *"It is here that the gravity of what is imminent will be grasped, and hope will be lost."*

All about them were dozens of scientist covered in personal protective equipment from head to toe; carefully, albeit hurriedly, darting around the lab inserting slides containing cultures from various pathogens under electron microscopes, while others observed the imaging on computer monitors and entered data into the system for analysis. An assistant walked past an enclosed 50'-by-50' glass cubicle containing numerous 36-inch Ovitraps used to snare and monitor the Aedes aegypti mosquito. Entomologist worldwide were looking to the U.S. for a means to rout the impending ruin. The lab assistant approached a scientist logging statistics and interrupted him.

"Dr. Mason, Director Cummings is on the line," she said visibly flustered. "He's been video conferencing with the directors from the Ministries of Health from, Taiwan, Saudi Arabia, Ontario, and New Zealand," she said unconsciously looking over the doctor's shoulder as she spoke. "As well as several members of the World Health Organization all morning sir. He was adamant about having an update ASAP."

She walked over to a 96-inch flat screen monitor mounted on the wall and turned it on. The various directors of health organizations from all over the world popped up on the monitor in an array of split screen images. From the looks of concern on their faces, they had indeed grasped the gravity of the situation. Ken-Dao Ying, the Director General of the Taiwanese Ministry of Health, spoke first.

"Dr. Mason, good evening sir."

Yes, it was only 9:20 am at the CDC building in Georgia, but in Taiwan not only was it evening, but the Taiwanese Ministry of Health had been working nonstop for over twenty-four hours. The Director-General paused and took a sip of ginseng tea.

"Please excuse my being abrupt doctor, but my staff and I have been working for the past twenty-nine hours going over the information that you have been disseminating. Frankly, we find it to be quite alarming," he said taking another sip of tea. "Director Cummings has informed us that you have discovered a disturbing new development." He reached for the stack of documents lying on the desk in front of him and put his reading glasses on. "It seems that the Zika virus has gone through an "antigenic drift," that is to say, that it has now mutated. And by your account, if your reports are correct... it has now merged with the HIV virus. If what you're saying is true Dr. Mason, then we are witnessing an "antigenic shift" with devastating consequences."

The Minister of Health from Saudi Arabia chimed in, "Dr. Mason this is Minister Al-Abassi. With the utmost respect doctor- what you are suggesting is impossible. The HIV virus cannot live outside of its human host for more than a few moments, and there must be a constant core temperature of 98.6°, plus or minus 2° doctor. So again, with the utmost respect, I am compelled to reiterate that what you are saying is at the very least, questionable doctor."

There was a loud murmur amongst the Ministers of Health and the members of the World Health Organization as Minister Al-Abassi stated what they believed to be scientifically impossible.

A scientist in a bio-hazard suit stepped out of the cubicle enclosure after being sprayed with the insecticide pyrethrin. Dr. Mason introduced her to the panel. She was the world's foremost entomologist. "My esteemed colleagues, please allow Dr. Hartford an opportunity to present our..." he hesitated and then said, "her findings to you," he said correcting himself.

"Gentlemen and lady," she said acknowledging Helen Shelor, the Minister of Health from Ontario Canada. "As many of you have noted in years past, we here at the CDC in Georgia have vigorously opposed the releasing of genetically modified vectors into the ecosystem, specifically here in America off of the Florida Straits," she said shuffling through her notes. "And while early testing showed promising results, we still believed that it was too early to declare the experiment a success." She logged into the most recent computer annals and brought the data up on the screen for all to see. "Unfortunately we were right. If you look at the graph here on the left side of the monitor you'll note that the genetically altered male of the "Asian tiger mosquito" started off as the solution that we all anticipated, and we immediately saw a marked decline in the female of the species but...," she cleared her throat and her manner became more subdued.

"We started to observe that the females that weren't killed after mating with the modified males began to have nymphs that adapted and evolved into a new species. A species capable of transmitting the HIV virus along with the Zika and West Nile virus. In our efforts to thwart one disease, we've created a new virus, a super-strain." She commenced typing the letters and numbers that would change the course of history. "The name of this super-strain is called CRF20 HIV, or as we've taken to calling it, CHIV2O, and thus far," she sighed, "it's proven to be resistant to all antiretroviral therapy."

As the words left her lips, the scientist in the lab, as well as those who were conferencing from the far reaches of the Earth, stood silent. Included in that group was John. Asherah walked to him and embraced him once again.

"There is still more you must see child."

As they traveled, Asherah was somber. The seconds that it took for them to traverse time seemed eternal. Then She spoke.

"Great God Jehovah, the giver of all life; I, the Word ask that You bring to ruin those bringing ruin to the Earth."

John could only speculate what the next stop held for him. He wouldn't have to wait long to find out.

"We are here child."

John looked around. He saw that they were on a ranch. The sky was serene and picturesque. It was a gorgeous day. Asherah asked John to walk with her. It wasn't as if he had a choice. After all, who could refuse the Word of God?

"Of course Mother," he said. "Where are we going?"

"You only need walk with me, My son. Your senses will apprise you."

It soon became clear what Asherah was referring to. John heard gunshots and smelled the scent of burning flesh as they rounded the corner of a barn. There in the center of the fields, cowhands were shooting livestock, except for the chickens which were gassed. One of the ranch hands used a bulldozer to push them all, cows, horses, pigs, goats and chickens into a huge fiery pit. The rancher and his ranch hands all had on a surgical mask, but still, they buried their faces in the crooks of their arms to ward off the unbearable stench. Standing there at the edge of the pit was Ariel accompanied by five other angels. They came to Asherah and kneeled.

"Mother, disease has laid low millions of every kind of species upon the Earth. Man in his quest to destroy the vermin of the air and crop has killed off the fish of the oceans and the birds of the air, but his plague continues. When will he become wise to the error of his ways?"

Asherah caressed the face of Ariel and gazed at the agitated faces of her other children.

"Children, why do you worry so? This will be the sixth cycle that the Earth has seen. Twice before has God brought man to the brink of extinction and thrice has the Earth bore witness to "The Great Dying." A time when all living things were destroyed. But fret not My little ones. The birds of the air, the creatures that walk, slither and crawl shall not perish away forever. Nor shall the creatures of the deep."

Ariel lifted his head.

"It is only the memory of man that shall be smitten from the Earth," Asherah said reassuring the young angel.

John could only think of his aunt and uncle as he listened to Asherah speak about man's imminent annihilation. The voices of the rancher's brought John back.

"Dylan, you and Madison, gon' inside and help your mama git' dinner on the table and see if she needs any help with Ethan," he said shoveling chicken carcasses that hadn't made it into the pit. "Me, Caleb and Josè will finish up out here."

Asherah led John into a modest but immaculately kept home. The sister and brother stopped at the front door and removed their cowboy boots.

"Ma!" Dylan the second to the oldest whispered quietly.

"In here son."

The two siblings walked into a room where their mother sat attending their younger brother. Lying in the room set up like a hospice, clinging to life was the Smith's seventeen-year-old son Ethan. Madison who was nineteen would often take up the role of surrogate mother. Their brother Ethan had been bedridden for two years, and the toll that it had taken on their mother was visibly palpable. She walked over to the nightstand next to the hospital bed and picked up the bowl of ice chips that were starting to melt and began to gently rub them over her brother's lips. He smiled and tried to sit up in bed, but his frail body was too weak. He had the dubious distinction of being one of the first cases in the United States infected with the mosquito-borne HIV. Madison ran her fingers through her mother's hair.

"Momma would you like me to start dinner?" she asked sympathetically.

"No Maddie, I have it. You've been working outdoors all day. I know you must be exhausted," she said rising from Ethan's bedside. But I think Dylan could use a hand getting your brother cleaned up darlin'." Dylan was already lifting his younger brother off of the bed to take into the bathroom and undress him.

Victoria Smith went into the kitchen and sobbed to herself quietly so that her three children wouldn't hear. She thought back to that day when her husband Lonnie and their four children were out doing the morning chores. Ethan went into the barn to give the horses fresh water. As he dumped the stagnant water out of a young colt's drinking trough the mosquitos scattered, all except the one that would infect him and alter his life forever.

The day that he first began to show symptoms were indelibly etched in her mind. May 25, 2032, Ethan was fourteen. As far as she knew her son had never had a girlfriend. He'd never even kissed a girl. Never smoked, did drugs or even had a beer, and here he was dying from AIDS. The tears flowed down her face as she asked

God why. The front door swung open. It was Victoria's husband, Lonnie.

"How's supper comin' along honey?" he asked kissing his wife on the cheek.

"Almost done dear," she replied smiling half-heartedly.

"Caleb," he yelled out to their oldest son. "Go on and set the table for your ma' boy."

The father walked into his ailing son's room.

"Hey tiger, how you doin' today?" he asked.

Ethan again tried to sit up in his bed. "I'm fine pa'. I feel a lot better than I did yesterday."

His father grabbed a pillow and eased it behind his son's back, careful not to brush up against the ulcers that covered his entire body. He opened up the eight ounce can of the high protein nutrient that the doctors had prescribed when Ethan began experiencing nausea and vomiting. He stuck a straw in the dense blend and put it up to his son's lips. When Ethan finished, Lonnie wiped his son's mouth clean and kissed him on the forehead. As his son nodded off to sleep, he slipped out to join the rest of the family for dinner.

John asked Asherah why? In his mind, he tried to justify the pandemic affecting Brazil and other regions of the world, but why America? Granted while

America isn't perfect, pedophilia is categorically despised and against the law.

"John, while man is vastly familiar with the seven deadly sins, did you know that there are some deadly sins that are unknown?"

John shook his head no.

"Yes, My son, there are many, but one that all of mankind suffers from at one time or another is apathy. If it does not affect their household than they are blind to the plight of their brothers, sisters, and neighbors.

John thought he recalled Satan mentioning something about apathy, but he wasn't sure.

Asherah embraced John once more and continued speaking, *"Since her inception, America has turned a blind eye to the injustices and atrocities of the world unless it benefits her interest."* She looked lovingly at John. *"But it is not America alone that is calloused. Come child there is more to see."*

Not long after their departure, Ethan would succumb to his illness, as would millions of others.

INTERVIEWING GOD

Chapter VI

John looked over his left shoulder past Asherah. From where the two of them were standing, he could see throngs of people running. The sound of heavy artillery and gunfire could be heard in rapid succession not far behind. The panicked shrills of the apes and the birds in the treetops overhead were barely audible above the sounds of war. John saw cattle, dogs, and humans, fleeing alongside one another; all seeking to escape the carnage.

"Mother where are we?" John asked after hearing the terrified villagers scrambling by speaking French.

"We are in the Democratic Republic of the Congo, My child. Come."

Asherah led him back in the direction of the scurrying villagers. As they neared the small standing shacks that were a little more than huts, the smell of gunpowder and death became overwhelming. John pinched his nose and followed Asherah into one of the residences. Inside of the poorly lit dwelling, John saw three soldiers standing over a young boy no older than thirteen, the three of them prompting the youth on as he raped a seven-year-old girl who had already been raped by several of the men. As John gazed upon the men, who stood there drinking, smoking marijuana, and laughing, he could make out the likenesses of demons. This time Asherah did not interfere, She only walked over to the young girl and kissed her forehead delivering her to death. When She did, the child's sobbing and tears ceased, and an angel appeared. He looked at the Queen Mother and said nothing. He cradled the child's soul in his arms like that of a loving father and departed.

"Let us leave here," Asherah said motioning for John to follow her outside. She pointed to the sky and asked, *"Tell me what you see child?"*

John squinted in the bright sunlight, but he saw nothing. And then Asherah spoke.

"Let him see My Lord: See what men whom have sight, but see naught. For they are indifferent, and they are blinded by greed, pride, lust, and wrath."

No sooner than the words had left Asherah's lips, the things that John came to see filled him with terror. There, in every portion of the sky were depictions of wars past and present. World Wars I and II. Images of mutilated men in armor from periods long before John was born. He saw men, women, and children being beheaded. Still more being burned at the stake. He turned away, albeit too late, as the aftermath of a suicide bomber unfolded in an open bazaar in Afghanistan. The limbs of mothers buying Naan for their families, as well as the torsos and extremities of children blown across the landscape as they waited to buy bags of sweet almonds and baklava with the little monies they earned doing chores.

"Do not look away, My son!" Asherah said. *"See what mankind has done to his brethren."*

But the images were far too disturbing and far too many for John to continue to watch. In every part of the Earth where there was no war, there was wanton violence. In all of the Earth, no part of humanity went unscathed. He lowered his head in dismay. It was then that Asherah again took pity on the child of man. As John stood there watching quietly, Asherah remembered the young boy who cowered in the closet while his father murdered his mother. She walked to him and caressed his face.

"My sweet boy, these things that I show you are not meant to castigate or cause you anguish. No, they are merely preparing you for the time when you will be forced to make a decision."

John was growing weary of hearing that he was being "prepared" for something or another. He had all but given up on inquiring as to what that thing was. While John mused to himself, Asherah knelt down and ran her fingers through the red soil of the African continent.

"Rise up- You, who were born of war. Show man the cost of his violent desires!"

The ground began to rumble and out of the depths of the Earth came a horse the color of blood. Upon that horse sat a woman whom Asherah called the "Daughter of Conflict." In her right hand, she held a mighty sword forged in flames.

Asherah called to the rider, *"Teruah, My heart, in all of the Earth there are wars and rumors of war, where have you been daughter?"*

The angel of war, the second horseman, or more accurately, horsewoman, dismounted from her steed. She bowed before taking Asherah's hand and kissing it.

"Mother, I have been observing mankind; he is occupied with the killing of the Earth."

She looked at John when she spoke, *"It is not enough that he has killed his brother. Nor that he has hunted many of the Father's creations into extinction, but his brutality and gluttony are ne'er satisfied, and they are only eclipsed by his fondness for war."*

John looked Teruah over. It wasn't as if anything would, or could, surprise him at this point. But here he was, staring at her for no reason in particular, except that is... she looked like a teenager no older than nineteen. How could she be one of the Four Horsemen of the Apocalypse? How could this young girl be the rider called War?

"Queen Mother, I don't..." Before John could finish his statement, Asherah spoke.

"Why do you find it unfathomable that she is the second Horseman child?" Asherah asked John who had a puzzled, if not dubious look on his face.

John quickly responded, "Look at her Mother. She looks younger than me!"

Asherah smiled, *"Man-child, why do you look with your eyes and not your mind?"* She asked, but Asherah knew the answer.

Too many had stopped believing in miracles. And with every one of man's technological advances, he believed less and less in God.

"Teruah, tell John the number of your year's daughter."

Teruah's answer was not what John expected.

"I am six thousand years old. I am older than death, pestilence, and famine."

85

"Okay, but that still doesn't explain why you look so young," he replied to Teruah, but it was Asherah who answered.

"It is because the attributes of war, are by definition, childish. If men were to become enlightened, they would begin to understand that violence is an unnecessary and rudimentary act."

Asherah was right. John recalled some of the fights that he had in his life, far too many were juvenile.

Teruah addressed Asherah, *"Mother at this very moment humanity is making war against the Earth!"* Her voice was filled with anxiety.

"Go My child. Make haste."

Teruah climbed up on her stallion and was off.

To John none of what Asherah and Teruah said made sense.

"Mother how can mankind go to war against an inanimate object?" John asked. "The Earth isn't alive," he said sounding all too sure of himself.

This time Asherah grabbed him forcefully. When She did, the winds rushed by them. When they halted, they were in Prague Oklahoma. It was nighttime, but there was a sizeable well-lit structure that stood out against the night's sky. It was a hydraulic fracking rig. The sound it emitted was disturbingly loud.

John covered his ears and shouted, "What's happening?" As he took a breath the pungent scent of the chemicals made him cough.

"What you see happening here is hydraulic fracking. This is how man is committing acts of war against the Earth," Asherah said, visibly angry. She held her hands palms up and recited another invocation. *"Husband, I ask that you pour out your bowl of anger, out into the Earth. It must be made known the price for destruction."*

John saw visions of the slaughtered bodies of elephants lying next to heaps upon heaps of tusk. Elephants senselessly killed for ivory. He saw logging operations and deforestation cut a wide swath across the planet. From the rainforest of the Amazon to the swamps of Louisiana, trees lie in waste.

Asherah spoke, *"How foolish that it is beyond the comprehension of mankind that not only is the planet living, but every creature, every plant in the earth, water, and in the air are connected to his very existence?"* She asked rhetorically.

For how could John answer for all of mankind, and even if he thought he had the answer, how could he justify putting humanity and the entire planet at risk for profit?

When their journey came to an end, John, again heard the sound of buzzing. But unlike their excursion to Brazil, the buzzing didn't grow louder, to the contrary, it became fainter. John looked up and noticed the sky was overcast and grey. There was a slight breeze, and the temperature felt cool on his face. He took a step and felt the ground give way as though it was muddy beneath his feet. He glanced down and to his horror saw what he thought was dirt, were actually bees... dead bees more precisely.

"Queen Mother, what's going on? I don't understand? Why are we standing in the middle of what must be hundreds of millions of dead bees?" he asked raising one of his feet in revulsion.

"I am showing you these things so that you begin to understand that not only is the Earth a living thing, but that man, the creatures of the Earth and the very planet itself indeed have a symbiotic relationship." Asherah bent down cupping a handful of the dead bees and said, *"Mankind's survival is dependent on his comprehending this."*

Asherah led John through the droves of dead insects to a clearing where She held her hand outstretched toward the terrain and said, *"Come."* Straightaway, on command, two small boulders pushed through the earth. *"Let us sit child,"* She said fixing her flowing gown underneath her as She sat.

"John, many times you have questioned what it is that you are being prepared for. And while the time has not yet come to tell you what that is, I can tell you that the day is growing near that your purpose will be revealed to you, and on that day you will have a choice to make. For now, that is all I will say."

Although Asherah offered no conclusive answer, her words, or the tone of her words that is, put John at ease. But his mind raced with the things he had seen and heard. John never fancied himself to be a tree hugger, but he was beginning to understand what Teruah meant when she said ever so anxiously that, *"At this very moment humanity is making war against the Earth!"*

INTERVIEWING GOD

Chapter VII

When Asherah and John reached Heaven, this time Asherah didn't escort John to the palace directly. Instead, She took him to a place in Heaven where multitudes of angels stood glancing out over the vista, enthralled as though they were watching television. John noticed at the forefront of this massive crowd sat angels with feathered quilled pens and scroll parchments. Asherah took John by the hand to show him what it was the throngs were looking at.

As they walked, the masses parted and knelt acknowledging the Queen Mother, the Word of God. When they got to the front of the crowd, John looked out and saw what had them all so absorbed. John could see not just images, but he saw that they were observing people on Earth going about their daily lives. Now what those daily lives consisted of depended on the person and the environment they lived in. In Greece, people in the streets were rioting and protesting the proposed "austerity measures." As John looked to his left, he saw a tranquil scene of a grandfather teaching his grandson how to bait a hook on a lake in the Catskills of upstate New York. Angels who saw their loved ones pointed and smiled, but not all had cause to smile. Some angels saw their loved ones in the midst of committing vile acts. In Mexico, there were numerous beheadings, as well as men and women being dismembered with chainsaws. In the US, a teenager walked into a school with an automatic weapon and began shooting his classmates as they sat and ate lunch in the school cafeteria.

John watched as North Korea launched nuclear missiles into the Sea of Japan. He observed several U.S. fighter jets conduct airstrikes in Mosul, Iraq. In South America, violence and civil war had gripped the people of Venezuela. But to humanity's credit, all was not death and despair. John witnessed inflatable rubber rafts with outboard motors flying the Greenpeace banner interfering with a Norwegian whaler. There were Doctors Without Borders donating their time and providing medical services all over the world. Churches were offering shelter and sanctuary to immigrants and refugees alike.

Firefighters were rushing into burning buildings. Mothers were preparing family meals. A Father was tossing a baseball to his son. Law enforcement officers worldwide were putting their lives on the line in the face of danger. Soldiers were at war endeavoring to save the lives of their fellow man and free them from oppression. The sights before him washed away John's earlier indictment of man being filthy and violent, John's mind raced as he thought.

"I knew it! Man can't be all bad," and while he was right, there was still more iniquity in the world than good. John just didn't know it.

"Mother, why are those angels sitting in front of the crowd writing?" John asked.

"They are scribes, My son. It is they who are obliged to record that which man is doing on the Earth," Asherah replied.

"But why? Doesn't God know everything that goes on?" John asked.

"Yes child that is correct," Asherah said smiling at John's naïveté. *"The scribes are recording man's acts so that they may be transcribed into the Book Of Life."*

Asherah proceeded to explain to John what the Book Of Life was. She knew John well enough to know what his next question would be.

"The Book of Life contains every deed that man has done since the beginning of time. Since the creation of Adam and Eve, there is not one man, woman or child whose actions are not recorded."

"But... doesn't God know.... everything that goes on?!" he repeated a bit antsy.

Asherah answered while She too looked out at Her offspring on the Earth, *"The Scribes do not keep records for God, My child. Man's doings are written down in the Book Of life so that his deeds shall be read back to him and his loved ones who plea for mercy on his behalf and for his passage into Heaven on the day of judgment. But that is only if they find reason to do so."*

"But why wouldn't someone's loved ones want them to experience all that Heaven has to offer?" John asked holding his arms open and waving them about as if he were a real estate agent showing a prime piece of property.

Asherah grew stern, while not antagonistic. She, the Word of God, knew that the time was growing nearer when John would have to choose, and She answered him in such a manner that he should feel the importance of what lies ahead as well.

"Because child, while man is selfish and only cares to do what satisfies the flesh…we in Heaven, we see all that you do. I, your Father, every angel in Heaven, and yes, your loved ones and the Christ who gave His life for you. We all see your filth. Whether it is in your questionable actions or in your salacious thoughts! We see it all. There is nothing that is hidden from us, and we are tasked with trying to find forgiveness for your immorality and impiety."

When Asherah finished what might be construed as a rant, a holy rant, but a rant nonetheless, She called for Sandalphina. Seconds later Sandalphina appeared.

"Yes, Mother?" she answered quietly.

She could see that her mother and John were both visibly upset.

"Take him to the Hall of Prayers," Asherah said before regaining her composure and walking off.

Sandalphina simply nodded and gestured for John to follow her. They arrived at another majestic edifice. This one resembled a great library. Outside there were more crowds. When John and Sandalphina entered the building, there were tens of millions of voices. At times, some were more audible than others.

Sandalphina whispered to John, *"Close your eyes and listen, brother."*

When John closed his eyes, he could hear people's prayers as clear as day. They were no longer unintelligible, to some degree anyway.

"Ten ni orareru watashi-tachi no Chichi yo, Minna ga seito saremasu yo ni."

John thought to himself, "They're speaking in Chinese."

Sandalphina corrected him, "No brother, they're praying in Japanese."

And there was more.

"Padre nuestro, que estás en los Cielos."

John marveled at the symphony of prayers that he heard in so many different languages.

"Baba Yetu uliye mbinguni."

Though he understood none of it, it was soothing nonetheless.

"Vater unser im Himmel, geheiligt werde dein Name;"

John listened quietly.

"Avinu shebashamayim yitkadesh shimkha."

"Отче нащ иже еси на небесех!"

So many languages, Spanish, Swahili, German, Hebrew. John thought that he may have even heard a Russian accent amongst the praying. But what stood out to John more than any of the other prayers was the Arabic that he heard.

"Bismila, ar-Rahman, ar-Rahim."

He was confused. In high school when they studied The Crusades or the Dark ages, he remembered that Muslims and Christians were at odds with each other on numerous subjects. One sticking point he vividly recalled, is that Muslims didn't acknowledge Jesus as the Son of God.

John asked Sandalphina, "What are they praying for?"

Sandalphina hesitated before answering, *"These prayers that you hear are the Lord's prayer. At least that is how many of them start out. But the prayers vary brother. It depends on the person and their desires. Some are praying for loved ones. Others are praying for health. While others pray for prosperity."*

As John deliberated in his head, he couldn't help but ponder, "Maybe God is right. Maybe we are really as selfish as He and the angels believe we are?"

When he turned to Sandalphina to ask a question, the words that came out of his mouth were about the thing that puzzled him the most about the prayers he heard in the hall.

"Sandalphina," he said. "I find it strange to hear Arabic in the Hall of Prayers. I mean, if Muslims don't believe in Jesus." He stopped for a second and considered his words. "I mean- we're in Heaven, and the Son of God is walking around getting an army ready for the next holy war. So, where do Muslims fit into this scenario?" he asked.

Sandalphina walked toward the exit and said, *"Come with me brother."*

The two of them exited the Hall of Prayers and began to walk in the direction of a garden that was surrounded by six buildings of religious worship. The six structures, although they appeared to form a circle, unbeknownst to John, they were aligned in in such a manner that if you were to draw a line from one to the other, you would see that each was a point in the Star of David. The first building, a church, while quite large seemed oddly out of place. At least as far as all of the other breathtaking sites that John had seen in Heaven. The word Catholicism was written on a sign that hung over the entrance of the church. Other then that, it was rather dull. Printed on a sign that hung on a temple was the word Buddhism. On another temple, the word Judaism. John spun around and saw the word Hinduism on the temple behind him. The last two places of worship facing one another, but a tad offset, was a Christian church and a mosque. Of all of the religious shrines, not one was ostentatious! In the center of the garden, John saw several men and women sitting and talking.

Sandalphina spoke, *"Brother, this is the Garden of Worship,"* she said taking a knee.

Sandalphina introduced them in no particular order.

98

"John this is Moses, the founder of Judaism. It was for him whom Almighty God parted the Red Sea so that the people of Israel would be freed from bondage. It is also he whom God gave the Ten Commandments so that man might have laws by which to abide." Sandalphina said rising and nodding toward Moses, *"This brother, is David, slayer of Philistine giant Goliath. David, The second King of Isreal. The poet who poured his heart out to our Father in the Psalms of the Old Testament."*

"David looks shredded," John thought to himself. "Not an ounce of fat on him."

Sandalphina then introduced the first of the three women that were sitting and conversing in the garden.

"This is the Devi or Goddess if you will . . . Kālī," Sandalphina said bowing her head acknowledging the Hindu Goddess.

The word Goddess was too much for John to swallow. The fact that the Goddess Kālī had four arms, which was startling in itself, and a hue as black as Sandalphina's, hadn't affected John at all. After his visit to Hell and meeting with Satan, John didn't think he would be fazed by anything that he saw. But the word Goddess was the straw that broke the proverbial camels back.

"What!" John exclaimed.

"Sandalphina, how is that possible? It goes against everything that my aunt and uncle have told me my entire life. The first commandment is, God is the only God. And to make it even more incredulous is, the Devi Kālī is sitting here talking to Moses. The one who brought us the Ten Commandments," John said putting his hands on his head as though his mind were blown.

But again John was mistaken, the first commandment given to Moses was, "You shall have no other gods before me." Before Sandalphina could reply, John interjected.

"I know it will all be revealed to me when the time comes."

He had heard that phrase, or a version of that phrase enough to recite it verbatim, or close enough to it.

Sandalphina introduced another woman whose head was veiled and wore a habit.

"This is St. Teresa of Ávila, or as our Father prefers to call her…St. Teresa of Jesús."

When Sandslphina introduced her, the nun curtsied quaintly.

"She was so devoted to our Father that he instructed Jesus the Christ to visit her daily for two years as to edify her

on the weight of the original sin to ease her suffering." Sandalphina paused looking at St. Teresa with compassion. *"But I think it was almost too much for her to bear."*

Sandalphina walked over to a man, and a woman that John assumed were a couple.

"John, this is Adam, the first of our Father's prophets. The one whom God tasked with naming all the creatures of the Earth. The one to whom after God, man owes his very existence."

She then turned to a woman that John could only describe as an exotic beauty.

"Is every woman in Heaven Gorgeous?" he wondered innocently.

"And this my brother, is Eve. The mother of mankind. The one to whom after God mankind owes their very existence. One of only two ne'er to be born from the womb of a woman. Adam, made from the dust of the Earth and Eve, fashioned from the rib of Adam. The first to be called wife."

It was now Sandalphina who fully bowed in front of Adam and Eve. The first of God's creations who God instructed her and all of the angels in Heaven to serve. Now while no one could argue that John was no theological scholar, he believed he knew enough to know that Sandalphina had omitted a crucial bit of information about Eve also being the first to commit sin.

Sandalphina made no attempt to correct John's presumptions because she knew, as did all of the other archangels, that Lucifer and the archangels that sided with him that fateful day were the first to sin against our Father. A day that was a source of grief for her and the archangels. Disregarding John's preconceived notion, Sandalphina pointed to one of the three remaining men that were in the group. She bowed her head to him as well.

"Brother, this is Shakyamuni. He is known by man as Gautama Buddha, the awakened one. The crown prince of the great Shakya kingdom. Because he forsook all of his Earthly wealth and status and sought out to find the solution to ending human suffering ... In him, our father is well pleased ."

The last two men were introduced in one breath. Concurrently so to speak.

"This is Rabbi Mukhayriq and his brother bonded by conflict, the Prophet Muhammad. May peace and blessings be upon him," Sandalphina stated showing respect to God's messenger.

As she finished introducing the last of the assemblage, John finally lets his thoughts drift to the elephant in the room. All of those that Sandalphina announced, with the exception of the Devi Kālī and the St. Teresa of Ávila...were Black. And no, not black like the color of Sandalphina's hue, black as in black-skinned. Also, just as arresting, was that none of them had wings.

"Just another question he'd have to get around to asking God at a later time," John told himself.

Sandalphina began spouting off the history of the two pious men as she had done with the others of the group, *"This brother is Rabbi Mukhayriq. It is he who fought side by side at The Battle of Uhud with his Muslim brothers. But it is not for that alone for which he is honored."* Sandalphina bestowed the words, *"And in him, our Father is well pleased.* Upon the Rabbi as well, she continued, *"Well pleased, in spite of the holy esteemed Rabbi disobeying the commandment; "Keep the Sabbath day holy," and choosing to fight alongside his Muslims brothers on the Shabbat, the holy Sabbath. Glory be to God, who pardoned him and granted him favor as he forsook the covenant of his religion to join with those of another faith to fight a common enemy; On that day, Jew and Muslim alike, as one. Thus in doing so, he exemplified the true meaning of brotherhood."* Sandalphina repeated, *"And in him, our Father is well pleased."*

The Prophet Muhammad embraced the Rabbi Mukhayriq and kissed him on both cheeks smiling and said the word *Akhee,* Arabic for, my brother.

Sandalphina smiled and greeted the Rabbi, *"Shalom."* She then greeted the Prophet Muhammad, *"Assalamu Alaikum."*

The sight of Jew and Muslim hugging one another and talking as brothers was a sight to see. Back on Earth, at least as far as John could recollect, there was always some news story about war in the Middle East over religion. John was only partially right. Most wars fought in the Middle East weren't over religion, but they were actually fought over the same causes as in any other part of the world; ethnic identity, land or resources. Or, as Satan gleefully stated, "An overinflated sense of pride and voracious greed." But make no mistake, God did have a problem with man killing one another in His name, or in the name of religion. But that, coupled with a host of other transgressions, was not why John had been summoned to Heaven. It was more ominous and urgent than that.

Then John heard something that he hadn't heard before. It was the voice of God speaking to him. Now to be clear this wasn't the first time God had spoken to John. God spoke to John frequently as He has spoken to all men. John was only becoming receptive now. What John didn't know was that Sandalphina, the

Rabbi Mukhayriq, and the Prophet Muhammad had heard God also. It was a simple but direct command.

"My children, come to Me."

This time Sandalphina found no need to inform John that God had summoned them. She knew that John had heard the Father for the first time in years. Inside she felt a sense of delectation. As the four walked to the house of God, the Prophet Muhammad began to address John's question that he had in the Hall of prayers. The one about God and the angels hearing the prayers of Muslims. The Prophet Muhammad placed his hand on John's shoulder, an atheist, and began to explain Islam to him.

"My brother," the prophet said calmly. *"When the malāk Gabriel,"* he stopped and translated the word "malāk" for John. *"When the "angel" Gabriel came to me and informed me that Allah would soon come to me and reveal the Quran to me, not only was I troubled; but I also feared others would believe me possessed."* He and the Rabbi both laughed out loud. *"Of course I could not understand why Allah, whose wisdom is infinite, would come to me with a novel religion,"* he said. *"I had been going to Mount Jabal al-Nour to pray and reflect in the cave Hira for years. When Allah came to me, He instructed me as he had done with all previous prophets that I was to*

105

spread His word in the Arab Peninsula and beyond to all that would incline their ears and heart to the word of God."

But the Prophet confessed that he still had doubt as to why God would not have him, and his people follow the religions of Christianity or Judaism. Before Muhammad could clarify his hesitation; the sound of hundreds of thousands of soldiers chanting and marching toward the garden made it impossible to hear anything being said. Anything except, *"Death, destruction, the end of man!"*

At the forefront of the battalions of angels was the Lord Jesus Christ. Walking beside Him were the Virgin Mary and Mary Magdalene. The two women who were with Jesus when He ascended into Heaven off the cross were now at His side sending Him off to war. John observed that Christ and every angel in His command were fully armored with helmet, shield, greaves covering their shins and tunics made of mail, but that was where the uniformity ended. Though Christ and His archangels carried swords, angels amongst the ranks carried a variety of weapons. Some carried clubs, while others marched with bow and arrow, and some among them were armed with javelins and slingshots. All of their weapons, John noted, were aflame. As the Lord Christ passed the four of them, Sandalphina, the Prophet

Muhammad, and the Rabbi Mukhayriq kneeled and bowed their heads. And yes, this time John also kneeled down and bowed.

After Christ had passed, John turned and saw the battalions separate into numerous divisions and march off into different houses of worship. As they did their chant now became a battle cry. *"Death, Destruction, The End Of Man!"* The four rose, but Sandalphina nor the two holy men made any mention of what they had all just witnessed.

The Prophet Muhammad picked up the conversation where he left off as if nothing happened.

"It wasn't until I ascended into Heaven and was able to look back on Earth- that I began to understand," he paused and said, *"Somewhat, the wisdom of Allah."*

He wanted to make it clear that he was well aware that no human being could ever begin to assume he or she knew the will of God. The Prophet went on.

"As I looked down on the Earth I saw that Jew and Arab could not be distinguished apart, one from the other. We are all children of Adam and Eve. All descendants of the Prophet Ibrahim, may peace be upon him."

"If I may say something brother?" the Rabbi Mukhayriq asked. The Prophet Muhammad nodded his head in approval. *"The reason is as it was when Cain slew Abel. The*

reason Eve ate the forbidden fruit. Man will never wholly capitulate to God's will. It is why Jehovah sent prophets from among each tribe of man so that He might save them." He then said under his breath, *"Sadly it is futile."*

The Prophet Muhammad resumed elucidating to John about the misconceptions of Islam, *"When I recited the words of the Quran as they had been dictated to me by Allah, it was to show the descendants of Ishmael, son of Ibrahim the way to enlightenment. The tribe of Isaac had the Torah, and for no other reason than the tribe of one brother, refusing to follow the religion of the other brother's tribe, we in our stubbornness, denied the religion of Isaac and they the religion of Ishmael."*

"But that's not it," John interjected. "The reason I was surprised to hear Arabic in the Hall of Prayers, isn't because I care which religion is better, Judaism, Islam or Christianity. I'm an atheist!" he said ardently. "It doesn't make a difference to me. If you want me to be totally honest?" he asked speaking to both men, "I was surprised because I thought Islam was religion based on a doctrine of violence," John stated.

The prophet Muhammad was extremely saddened by John's statement. He lamented the point that many of his words had become a tool of manipulation and propaganda for men who wanted to further their own agenda. And while Islam being used as a vehicle to propagate violence immensely burdened the Prophet Muhammad, he recognized that men throughout history had used religion to their benefit. He and others in Heaven watched as slave masters used Christianity to enslave Africans for centuries in America, and how conveniently Christian and Jew forget the Spanish Inquisition. Not only were Muslims and Jews ordered to convert to Catholicism or be exiled, but thousands were tortured and murdered in the name of Catholicism. And yes, even Catholics were unjustly persecuted after their neighbors bore false against witness them; accusing them of being heretics, using the church to exact vengeance on the guiltless. Catholicism. The religion of King Ferdinand the II, and Queen Isabella I of Castile.

"No, no, no brother that assumption is false," the Rabbi Mukhayriq put his hand up correcting John's conjecture. *"I was there when my brother Muhammad instructed his followers on the duties concerning jihad. Yes, it is true that he instructed those of his tribe to kill the unbelievers wherever they found them and drive them out where they sought to expel them from the holy places."*

The Prophet Muhammad completed the last of that decree. *"For the sin of disbelief in God is greater than murder,"* the prophet said. *"But,"* the rabbi continued, *"Muhammad and his people along with the Jews of my tribe were under attack by Abu Sufyan ibn Harb and the Meccans who were ruthlessly trying to stamp out the worshiping of the one God Jehovah!"* the Rabbi said vehemently.

"And though neither Jew nor Muslim declares Christ as the son of God, we jointly believe that he is a divine prophet of Allah," Muhammad said. *"And,"* the prophet Muhammad added, *"Nowhere in the Quran do I advocate for senseless violence or the harming of innocents."* And as a final note, the prophet declared, *"Nor do I condone suicide in the name of jihad!"*

As they neared God's, palace, the Rabbi said to John, *" John, whether man is Christian, Jew, Muslim or any of the faiths that do or do not laud the name of Yahweh or Yeshua; the common thread is, and should always be love. The love of one's brothers and love for all of God's creatures."*

The Prophet Muhammad looked at John and said, *"This is where we leave you, brother. Assalamu alaikum,"* he said bowing to John.

The rabbi Mukhayriq also bowed and said, *"Shalom."*

The Rabbi's and Prophet's word's about love being the foundation of all religions resonated with John, *"The common thread is, and should always be love."*

Chapter VIII

The two men went on their way as Sandalphina and John entered the Palace. John could hear chatter coming from the Throne Room. When John and sandalphina stepped inside, the room grew quiet. God spoke.

"Ah, there you are children. John, did you enjoy the Hall of Prayers?" God asked smiling.

Enjoy wasn't a word that John would have used. Somewhat informative? Yes. Even soothing as John recalled. Nevertheless, John was relieved that a few of his questions had been answered, but yes, there were still more.

Sandalphina took her seat as John sat on the floor and crossed his legs.

"Father," John said looking at God wide-eyed the way a young child looks at their parent when they're in need of answers beyond their ability to comprehend. "The Prophet Muhammad explained to me in detail the misconceptions that I had about Islam. And I'll admit I feel a little differently now, but, and this is a huge but," he said, "There's something that I have to ask you." John carefully choose his next few words, "All of the Prophets in the Garden of Worship were Black. Not that there's a problem with that...." he said, again pausing. "But if Adam and Eve were Black- then how did we get Asians, Hispanics and White people like myself?" he asked. "I'm just saying it's all a little perplexing," John added.

The angels didn't know what to make of John speaking to God as though He was an ordinary being, but God took no offense to John's line of questioning. On the contrary, God reveled in the familiarity. He wanted His children to speak to Him as though he was their father, which He is. God rose up from His throne and walked over to John.

"Stand up child." God leaned in and uttered just above a whisper, *"I heard Asherah tell you that She was more powerful than I. Imagine that- I'm God,"* God jokingly said. *"I allow her that. Mankind has a phrase; I believe it goes 'Happy wife, happy life.' Well, I've been known to say "Happy Word, happy world."* God roared with laughter.

Who knew God had a such a sense of humor.
"Take a walk with Me child."

It was another beautiful day in Heaven.

"Not to sound ungrateful," John stated, "but are there ever any bad days up here?" John asked God.

112

"Yes, John, there are some difficult days in Heaven, but bad days in Heaven are catastrophic on Earth my child. However, that is a matter for another time."

God approached John and placed His hand on John's head. As He did the scene around the two quickly changed.

"I need not transport your flesh to a time or place. I am the Lord God. Time has no sovereignty over Me. It is I, and I alone who created the notion of time. I need only think and it is. I am both Eternal and Unbounded. Look, My child," God said.

Everywhere John looked there were different species of animals. But, he hadn't seen these animals anywhere prior, at least not that he could remember.

"John, these creatures that you see before you have been hunted to extinction by man. They only exist here at this time in the Garden of Eden."

As the scene continued to morph John saw species of the sea.

"Father, are all of these species extinct as well?" he asked looking up at the many species of birds that man had driven into extinction, either by hunting them or destroying their natural habitats.

"Yes, My child. Every creature you see here has been erased from the face of the Earth, but that is only

part of the reason I brought you here. I also come here because it pleases Me to see My creations alive and thriving as I intended."

God walked over to a tree that grew in the center of the garden. John thought that he had seen the tree somewhere before, but he couldn't put his finger on it. Then it came to him as he walked nearer to get a better look.

"Father, is this the tree that Sandalphina told me was forbidden to eat from?" John asked inquisitively.

"No John, this tree is the progeny of that. The tree you observed in Heaven is the tree of Knowledge of Good and Evil."

God knelt and scooped up a handful of dirt and began to form the figure of a man as John looked on in amazement. God then put his lips to the mouth of the being that He forged from the earth. Filled with God's breath the man promptly came to life.

"John, this is a recreation of Adam. Tell Me, My child, what color is the earth that I have fashioned Adam from?" God asked John.

John looked for a moment and then answered, " It's dark brown- almost black," he conceded.

"Indeed child," God replied. *"The first man. The father of civilization. Your earthly father had the same*

114

black hue as the earth that he was fashioned after. This is what man has failed to grasp," God declared with torment in his voice. *"When you kill your enemies in war, you are in fact killing your brothers."* God set Adam down beside the tree. *"But more than that,*" God said looking around, *"Every creature that soars through the sky, every creature that walks upon the Earth and swims in the oceans- I have formed them from the earth just as I did Adam."*

The Creator looked around with pleasure at the creatures that no longer walked the Earth, but would forever exist in the Garden of Eden, free to graze, swim and fly about. Fulfilling the grand design in which they were created for. But man, in his ignorance or perhaps arrogance believes that he is the only species on Earth with a significant purpose.

"Think of the earthworm child. To the unknowing, it is little more than a lure for fish. But see how it goes about fertilizing the soil. Feeding the vegetation from the cast it excretes. Burrowing through the soil creating crevices for the rain to permeate the Earth," God said beaming, digging his hand into the earth once more and coming up with a handful of earthworms.

But John had become distracted. He was watching a tiger crouching and stalking what appeared to be a mutation of a deer and zebra. God informed John that the strange animal that he was observing was called a Quagga. It had been hunted to extinction in the late nineteenth century. The tiger stalking the Quagga wasn't just any tiger, it was a Javan tiger last seen in the wild in the late twentieth century. God and John both looked on as the tiger leaped into action, pursuing the Quagga as it darted through the garden trying to elude the big cat. But the tiger rapidly gained ground until finally, the mighty predator slapped the Quagga's hind leg causing it to stumble. When it did it, the hunt was over as quickly as it had begun. The tiger bit down on the animal's neck suffocating it. John was awe-struck and simultaneously puzzled. "Why had God allowed the tiger to kill the Quagga?" he wondered.

God placed the handful of earthworms in a grassy patch and reached down into the earth once more and began to shape another figure. His hands moved like that of a master artisan. When God was finished, John saw Him cuddling the body of a small, lifeless Quagga.

"This is but a foal, My child. A youngling," God said placing His lips on the snout of the young Quagga, and just as He had done with Adam, He blew life into the creature. The foal squirmed and lept from God's arms wobbling on its tiny hooves joining the other Quaggas in the zeal. John felt his eyes tear up, and then the

tears, tears of joy started to run freely down his face. John felt a bit embarrassed.

"Sheesh, look at me crying like a baby," he said.

But God wiped away John's tears and spoke, *"You need not be abashed. You are being shown what none but the angels in Heaven have witnessed.You are becoming aware that every creature on this planet is created by My hand from the dust, and is given life by My breath, so it is that all things are as one. The birds of the air, the creatures of the deep, man and every species that walks the Earth. You all have a reciprocal connection. The Quagga feeds the tiger, who is but one of the predators whose tasks is to keep in check the species that eat vegetation, ensuring that the planet does not become barren; And thus all life may thrive. And though I have given man authority over every species of the Earth, ne'er forget that even a creature such as the lowly earthworm is a part of that cycle. No creature's role is more important than another's ."*

God walked back to the tree where Adam was still seated. He picked a small, purple, fruit up off the ground. He split the fruit in two, giving one half to John and the other to Adam. John was still hesitant hearing Sandlphina's adamant warning in the back of his mind.

"Our Father has said to all who are in Heaven that we may eat all that we wish, but we must not eat from that tree. The tree of knowledge of good and evil." He quickly brushed the thought out of his head.

"Who am I to question God?" he thought.

John had no idea, but he was no longer the atheist who arrived in Heaven days ago. To John's delight when he bit into the fruit, the taste of blueberries and cream filled his mouth.

"Quite delicious isn't it child?" God asked.

"Uhm-hmm," John said taking another bite of the fruit.

"It's an African star apple," God said. *"Once I found that Adam and Eve had eaten of the forbidden fruit, I removed it from the Garden of Eden and relocated it to Heaven where it would be secure from the grasp of mankind. But it was too late. The damage had been done. Man now knew Evil."*

God walked over to the tree where Adam, or more precisely the recreation of Adam was sitting and waved His hand over his head. To John's astonishment, the replica of Adam immediately turned to dust. John threw the rest of the star apple on the ground and spat what he had in his mouth out while wiping his hands on his pants.

"You see John, I knew that Satan would lead man astray. First by deceiving Eve. Leading her to believe that I wanted her and Adam to remain injudicious. Adam being of weak mind and flesh, despite My instructions, followed Eve in her iniquity," God said. *"But it wasn't so. I intended to give Adam and Eve knowledge daily... as bread,"* God stated. *"Weaning them as a mother suckles her babe. Fortunately, I intervened before they consumed enough of the fruit for the knowledge to drive them mad."*

John heard rumbling in the brush behind him and God. He spun around to see four large birds sprinting quickly towards them. They were covered in black colored plumage with stunted white wings, brown underbellies, and oversized beaks. Each one standing nearly three feet tall ran to God, jumping about making frenzied clucking sounds, raspy and deep. Something like a cross between a turkey and one of those annoying squeak toys a child plays with John noted.

John instinctively looked around for a stick to pick up to defend himself. Ready to bash every one of the bird's skulls in if need be.

God raised His hand and bellowed, *"No!"*

John froze in his tracks.

"These birds you see here are called Dodo birds, My child. Extinct since the late seventeenth century."

God dispersed some of the star apples to the flightless birds who then went on their way squawking and clucking as they made haste back into the depths of the garden.

"You could have easily killed them, My son. Just as the sailors who first encountered them. Arrogantly renaming them the Dodo bird because they had no fear of man," God said.

"So what were they called before?" John asked.

"Adam named them Habi's," God replied.

"A Habi? Yeah, that sounds a lot better than a Dodo bird," John said nodding his head.

The creator resumed where He had left off, *"It was My intentions to instruct Adam and Eve on the difference between good and evil. Those teachings coupled with wisdom and knowledge would have ensured man a long and prosperous existence. But Adam and Eve having eaten from the star apple caused all of mankind born from that day forward to be born in sin and condemned to death. Picture if you will, the children in their adolescence who are now exposed to wanton violence, murder, fornication and every form of wickedness before they know Me or the Word of God."*

As they walked, a swarm of thousands of beautiful blue butterflies flew from one tree to another.

"The more knowledge man acquired, the less he heard My voice," God said as the scenes transformed again.

This time John saw images of Adam and Eve leaving the Garden of Eden naked. At the entrance of the garden stood an angel with a flaming sword barring the two from ever returning. Remorsefully, God slaughtered two of the beloved creatures that He had given Adam charge over and clothed he and Eve in the animals' skins. While John watched, he saw that God still mercifully counseled the two of them. He also observed the recompense for Eve's disobedience. After giving birth to Cain, in her hubris, she declared, "With God's help, I have created man." God scarcely acknowledged his daughter's foolish words. However, He saw to it that when she delivered Abel, it would be in the throes of agony. But God had yet to be satisfied. To John's horror, he witnessed Cain take his plow and repeatedly hack his brother Abel to death-disemboweling him in the process.

God turned to John, *"This was when I first began to regret My giving man the will to choose his own destiny."*

God then told John that Adam and Eve would live for another nine hundred and thirty years; bringing forth fifty-six offspring.

"But unfortunately, even after I exiled Adam and Eve from the Garden of Eden, mankind would not learn from the sins of their forefathers. Furthermore, they would be influenced by the Nephilim, the fallen angels I have told you about. The Nephilim would have intimate knowledge of the daughters of man, and the women of Earth would give birth to half-demons and giants. To Lucifer's amusement, his sycophant's would influence man so that they were full of violence and turpitude. I would have to cleanse the Earth once more."

God showed John Noah and his kin going about building the ark. When Noah and his family were done, the Heavens opened up, and it began to rain. At first, the people of Noah's clan paid no attention to the rain which started as a trickle; they mocked Noah, laughing and calling him a fool. But after the tenth day, when the storm had not subsided, and the waters began to besiege the Earth, their fate dawned on them. The multitudes of the wicked and the nonbelievers commenced to pounding furiously on the sides of the ark as the waters swelled and the oceans and seas became one. Those who did not drown immediately were set upon and devoured by sharks, whales, giant squid and all other flesh eaters of the sea. Species who were natural enemies in the deep, now acted in concert to do God's bidding and finish man from the Earth. John saw the creatures swim about in a feeding frenzy feasting on the flesh of mankind. The black waters quickly turned blood red. The only sound to be heard beside the torrential downpour was the screams of the hapless.

God, unmoved by their pleas spoke, *"It was then that I decreed that man should not live for nine generations henceforth. Because of his waywardness, from that day forward no human would live to see more than four generations of their descendants,"* God declared as the scenery changed once more. *"Look here, My son. The answer to your query."*

When John glanced, he saw a beautiful city. There were no longer flood waters. Instead, there were men at work throwing straw and wood inside a kiln feeding the fire and stirring the embers. Others carried bricks made of clay, placing them one by one inside the hearth with a long-handled wooden paddle. John didn't know it, but it had been nearly one hundred and six years since the great flood, and the human species resolute had rallied back from the verge of destruction, as robust as ever. Yes, indeed, it appeared that mankind had rebounded and was now thriving on the plains of Shinar.

John saw that in the center of the city, the residents had erected a soaring tower. A tower that stretched so far into the sky he had to put a hand up to his eyes to try and see the zenith. Arching back, John looked up and said, "It has to be at least a hundred stories." Squinting because of the glaring sun, he added, "And they're still going at it."

There were vendors peddling wares and goods and young boys tending to goats. Young girls and women were kneading bread, busy preparing meals for the men who were hard at work constructing what could only be described as a monumental metropolis. The entire community seemed to be laboring as one.

"I think they got the message, Father," John said to God.

"One would think so My child. But look closely," God answered back.

When John looked, he saw a man being carried from out of the base of the tower.

"That is Nimrod," God said. *"He is the great-grandson of Noah. He has declared himself king of Shinar. He has also told the people that they need not go forth and be fruitful. Foolishly*

decreeing they should build a prodigious tower as to prop themselves up against Me," God retorted. *"Now look closer My son,"* God said.

John continued observing the self-proclaimed king and the people of Shinar. That's when he saw them again; demons whispering in the ears of men. Two stood by Nimrod giving him counsel while other demons were mingling about the populace, murmuring to the foreman who urged their men to keep up the pace. For the demons knew what the men did not. God was here! John could see the demons pointing up at the sky instructing the men to build higher.

"But why Father?" John asked. "What do the demons have to gain by building a skyscraper?" he asked bewildered.

It was only after God explained the reason why they were building the edifice that John shook his head in disappointment.

"Satans minions are attempting to gain entry into Heaven with man's help. They have promised Nimrod wealth, power and oneness with Me if they would do so. Sadly, the descendants of Noah have not learned from the errors of their ancestors," God stated.

With a wave of His hand, the Heavens again opened up, and this time when they did... lighting

125

came down striking the demons who feverishly sought to hide amongst their unwitting co-conspirators. As the lightning struck them, they were immolated into smoke and ash. The people of Shinar ran for their lives, now calling on the very God they imprudently betrayed. From the Heavens, a flash of light tore through the sky. A light so brilliant it dulled the sun. Followed by the crack of thunder as lightning struck the tower reducing it to rubble. John covered his ears from the sound that one could only liken to the explosion of a bomb. The people fell to their knees and began to beg the creator.

"Jehovah have mercy on us. We beseech thee, Father... God of our ancestors. We are but sheep lost in the wild in need of a shepherd." They implored God lying prostrate, "Please, Father forgive us!"

Hearing their pleas, God compassionately said, *"Enough."*

When he did, the lightning ceased. Perhaps it was that man was only a quarter of his numbers before the great flood? Possibly it was that man had again merely been lead astray by the serpent? Maybe it was a combination of the two? Whatever the reason, the Almighty saw it fit to spare the inhabitants of Shinar.

Then God spoke, *"From this day forward you shall go about the Earth as I have intended. You shall be fruitful and fill the Earth with your progeny who will profess that I the Lord God am most merciful. Everywhere that you settle you shall build altars and bring forth the first of your crops to Me. The best of your livestock shall also be sacrificed to Me, the Alpha and the Omega. In all that you do, you shall glorify the name of Jehovah. But,"* God said, *"So that mankind will forever remember the happenings of this day; I will see to it that history will not forget the city of Shinar in the land of Babylon."* God then said ominously, *"And ne'er shall you. Hereafter you shall speak in tongues foreign from one to the next so that mankind shall ne'er again conspire against I, the Lord God. As long as man shall walk the Earth his words will be as babble to one another. And thus The Tower of Shinar will be forever known as the Tower of Babel."*

The people of Babel split into groups that spoke the same language. John understood none of it, but he didn't understand the Hebrew they were speaking before God cursed them with languages unfamiliar to one another. The small groups began gathering up their individual belongings and other items they would need for their journey. As the people of Babylon dispersed, John saw the features of the people beginning to evolve over time. But that wasn't all John noticed. He also saw that the Earth's land mass was no longer a complete sphere as it once was. It had now broken into the five continents, and man, determined, adapted to the continent in which he settled. In colder climates, his skin lightened. His broad nose now became thin. The color of a man's iris would also be affected by the environment in which he resided. The colors blue and green absorbed more light in colder regions.

God spoke again, *"As a reminder to humankind, I have given My children of Asia eyes like few others, for naught but to confound man and remind him that I alone am the Chief Architect."*

As the scenes began to fade away, images of the near future emerged. John could see nations that were formerly one tribe, now building armies to war against one another. Not only that, the demons that had scurried away at the sight of God had returned to finish their dirty work upon the Earth. John just shook his head. While God had answered his question about race, John was sure many bible thumping Christians would have a difficult time accepting the fact that all of mankind had begun in Africa. John was exhausted, mentally and spiritually.

"I don't understand why you permit us to go on Father?" John asked disheartened. "At every turn, we fall back to our old ways," he said.

But John's question was pointless. How could he, or any human fully grasp the love God has for man? It would be impossible. How could mankind wrap their head around the fact that an omnipotent, omniscient God still loves us despite knowing we would continue in immorality and impenitence?

God answered John in earnest nonetheless, *"It is as it has always been. I afford mankind the choice and the chance to move away from wickedness because I love you from time indefinite to time indefinite. That is why I send My angels and prophets to guide you thus giving man an opportunity to repent. Believing that man is redeemable, I sent My only son to die for your sins."*

As God went on speaking, and everything faded away, John and God stood where they had been all along... the Throne room.

"But it is all for naught," God said. *"Now it is time for you to rest My child. In the morrow, Asherah has more to show you."*

Chapter IX

For the first time since his arrival in Heaven John barely slept. That night he tossed and turned relentlessly. The thought of mankind hunting animals into annihilation along with the sight of the helpless, although rebellious people of the flood o' Noah, drowning or being eaten alive by the creatures of the deep, occupied his thoughts as well. And if that wasn't enough, in the back of his mind was the realization that while God is compassionate, when the time came, He would handle His business like no one else could. But John, like many people, tends to overlook the verses in the bible where God has slain babies and destroyed entire cities. Not to imply humans didn't have it coming, but still, those thoughts and more were wreaking havoc with John's "REM" sleep.

John woke up momentarily and muttered, "What a waste." But somewhere inside him, the belief that there had to be an answer prodded at his subconscious. If man's redemption was a lost cause, then why had God brought him here in the first place? As John finally drifted off to a sound sleep, he dreamt of his mother. Though John thought of his mother often, it had been years since he had dreams about her. It was as though she came to reassure him that everything would be alright. That next morning John awoke to the sound of Sandalphina's voice. She was gently shaking him.

"Wake up brother. It's morning. Our Father and the Queen Mother are expecting you," she said standing over him.

John got up from the grass and walked over to the fountain. He had made this his daily routine. Splashing water on his face, and cupping his hands together, he took a drink to quench his thirst. John then took another sip of water and swirled it around in his mouth before spitting it out. John paused for a second. He could feel that something was different. He couldn't put his finger on it, but it was eerily quiet since Christ had left with His army. Gone were the sounds of the legions of angels chanting for the destruction of mankind. John also noticed that the angels who had been observing man from the precipice of Heaven were absent as well along with the angelic children and infants who were usually playing outside in the sun under Heaven's blue sky.

John and Sandalphina entered the Throne Room to an audience of God's inner circle clothed in black robes. That is, everyone except for God Himself, who was draped in a pristine white tunic as always. God and those in the room greeted John with the customary salutations just as they had any other time, but unbeknownst to John, this was an unprecedented event. When all were done welcoming John, God informed him that his days in Heaven were coming to an end.

"In fact, it is the end of days for all of mankind," God said to John rather monotonously.

"I don't understand," John said. "I thought that I was being brought here this morning for the Queen Mother to take me on another journey and show me a few more things so I could get a better understanding of what's going on," John blurted out.

He then began to ramble as the severity of what was happening finally became evident.

"Look, God," John said arrogantly addressing the Most High. "I had a horrible nights sleep! So please forgive me if I appear a little less then amicable this morning. Not only did Sandalphina wake me up at the crack of dawn," John glimpsed over at Sandalphina and said, "Sorry." He then continued, "But I haven't had a chance to eat breakfast yet, and now you drop this bomb in my lap. And not just any bomb- the end of the world bomb!" John said taking a step back as the thought of running out of the Throne Room briefly crossed his mind.

God put His hands together interlocking His fingers before addressing John. That nuance, however reserved, made it apparent to all in the room that God had grown weary of John's antics, and the manner in which he spoke to John was a further indication of that impatience.

"Child, when I summoned for you, I, Asherah and Sandalphina made it clear that you were here for a purpose. Now the time has come for you to be made aware of that purpose," God said sternly.

John looked at Sandalphina and Asherah for help, but no one in the Throne Room dared to speak. God waved His hand signaling for an angel to enter the room. In came an angel carrying a large scroll. He wore a hooded robe that concealed his wings and shrouded his face. He then broke open the parchment which had been sealed with a drop of the blood of Christ and commenced reading from it. His voice filling the room as he did, *"Glory be to Jehovah, the Alpha, and the Omega."*

As the angel continued, the archangels rose from their thrones and prostrated themselves in front of the throne of God and recited a portion of the same prayer as did those tortured souls in purgatory.

"In the name of Jehovah, the Beneficent, the Merciful, all praises be to Jehovah, Lord of the universe, the Beneficent, the Merciful. Master of the day of judgment. It is You alone whom we worship, and to You alone whom we beseech for help. Keep us on the straight path. The path of those of whom You bestow Your favor. Not of those who go astray, nor of those who incur Your wrath."

The archangels wailed at the feet of God. The sight of them lying flat on the Throne Room floor outstretched, face down, was enough to scare any human being, but Sandalphina and the other archangels crying, pleading for God to have mercy, terrified John!

The angel read on, *"Glory be to the Christ Jesus. The firstborn from the dead who loosed mankind from their sins by means of His own blood. He has gone to the Earth to bring war to mankind, and all the nations of the Earth shall fall away because of Him. To the congregations of man, I give you these warnings. You say that you are alive in God and Christ, but you are dead to Him that knoweth all things. You are neither hot nor cold, but lukewarm and the Lord God shall vomit you out of His mouth! You who love riches more than you love morality. Now, look! The Christ is coming from the clouds, and every eye will see Him, and all the nations of the Earth will suffer because of Him."*

And then, suddenly, to John's delight, at least for the moment, the archangels ceased their prayers, and the angel who read from the scroll stood quietly as well.

"Whew, I'm glad that's over," John said, but it was far from over.

A red mist filled the room and in came four creatures saying, *"Holy, holy, holy is Jehovah God, the Almighty who was and who is and who is coming."*

The first creature resembled a lion. The second looked like a bull. The third appeared to be human... almost, and the last had the countenance of an eagle. Each was a monstrosity and had a ring of soulless eyes about its head which never blinked. Six wings protruded from their backs, and when the creatures spoke, they spoke as one, repeatedly saying, *"Holy, holy, holy is Jehovah God, the Almighty who was and who is and who is coming."*

John didn't know it, but these four aberrations were representations of the four corners of the Earth that man had all but devastated: The eagle representing the north, the bull the south, the figure of the man, the east, and the lion, the west. All four now cried out against mankind. Begging God to remove man from the face of the planet. Sandalphina and the others began their chant once more, louder than before.

"In the name of Jehovah, the Beneficent, the Merciful, all praises be to Jehovah, Lord of the universe, the Beneficent, the Merciful. Master of the day of judgment. It is You alone whom we worship, and to You alone whom we beseech for help. Keep us on the straight path. The path of those of whom You bestow Your favor. Not of those who go astray, nor of those who incur Your wrath."

Asherah got up from her throne and walked over to John. She wrapped her arms around him and pulled him close.

"You need not fear, My child. Though Christ is the first to be raised from the dead, those that believeth in Him, through our Lord God, shall be granted everlasting life," Ashera said comforting John as She transported the two of them.

When they came to a stop, John could smell the overwhelming stench of death once more. He looked around and saw the sick lying in the street. Black splotches oozing pus and blood covered their skin. Some of the men had their faces covered as they carried dead bodies, tossing them into piles, where other men would then come and pick them up to be burned. The infirmed suffered from delirium and other mental disorders which perhaps contributed to their lack of control of their bodily functions. For everywhere one looked, men dropped their trousers in public, while women lifted their skirts, forgoing dignity, they squatted and defecated in the streets. Some of the afflicted put filthy rags to their mouths, coughing up thick mucus filled blood clots. John looked on in horror as some of the city's residents bled from every orifice of their body. It was more than he could stomach.

"Mother where are we?" John asked holding his nose.

"This is the beginning of the Rapture, My child,"

This was Germany in the year 1349. The Great Pestilence or the Black Death as it came to be called, had Europe and most of the world in its grip and it would be another four years before the plague ended. When it was over, close to two-thirds of the Earth's population would be decimated. There were myriads of people praying in the streets. They had no choice. The plague had left no one unscathed. Priest and their entire clergy had succumbed to the disease. From a side alley, John saw a parade of more than a hundred men marching through the streets half-clothed, holding a bible in one hand and a whip in the other, beating themselves bloody, quoting scripture as they trudged along in a single file.

"The Rapture?" John asked. From what I understand, and what I've read on the occasion I happened to take a look at the bible, then the rapture occurs, two people would be in the middle of a conversation, and out of nowhere, one person, the righteous one that is, would be whisked off to Heaven leaving the other person on Earth to face judgment," John said feeling pretty sure of himself.

"That is precisely what you see before you child," Asherah said. *"But in the mind of man, the flesh would ascend to Heaven. But… that is in the mind of man. What God has dictated is that the vessel shall be left on Earth, and the spirit shall join the faithful awaiting the second coming of Christ,"* Asherah answered. *"You see some who are afflicted tending to the ill? Both those who are ministering and those that are being attended to are seeking death, but it will not yet come."*

"But why? What has mankind done to deserve this?" John asked. "This is the middle ages. Men aren't technologically advanced enough to do damage to the planet, so what's the reason they're being punished for now?" he asked reluctantly, not really wanting to know the answer.

Asherah faced John and said, *"Vanity, lust, greed. Seeking to be one with God, My husband. The same as it was and always is,"* She began walking toward another section of the city with John following closely behind her. *"Those who proclaim themselves keeper's of the word of God have grown wealthy under the pretense of religion. So do not be bereaved because of them, for there are none who are innocent here."* Asherah then pointed, and said, *"Look!"*

When John turned his head in the direction that Asherah was pointing, he saw men garbed in armor dragging families kicking and screaming from their homes.

"Where are they taking them, Mother?" John asked.

Seeing the children being hauled through the streets made him want to intervene.

"Come and see child. Come and see what more atrocities man is capable of," Asherah replied.

The pair walked down a passageway leading to winding stone steps lit by torches that led into a dungeon which had three large bronze crosses hanging over the entrance. One representing The Father, the other The Son, and the last The Holy Ghost. The guards took their directives from priest who answered directly to the Catholic church. These so-called men of God ordered the torture of the innocent in the name of religion. The priest stood by and watched as the guards submerged the hands of young children in boiling oil, and tore off the finger and toenails of other young children until they bore false witness against their parents while screaming in agony. Men who lay on the rack were pulled apart by the ankles and wrist until the sound of cartilage popping and bones cracking made some who were forced to watch faint. Adding insult to injury, they were forced to endure the taunts of their captors who mocked them yelling, "Confess Jew! Confess that you have called down a plague on the good Catholics and Christians of our Lord Jesus Christ!"

The women fared no better. Their breast and genitals were mutilated and burned with torches until they too admitted to the ludicrous charges brought against them. And yes, they also falsely accused relatives and friends, hoping by doing so they would escape with their lives. Those who were fortunate enough to avoid the cruelty were burned at the stake and death came promptly.

John walked past Asherah and exited the dungeon saying, "Enough! I've seen enough."

Asherah made no attempt to stop him, for there was more to see. Back on the streets of Mainz, Germany, John witnessed acts that would reinforce

Asherah's point citing man's greed. German merchants emerged from their shops and viciously attacked Jewish business owners under the guise of religious duty. Their schemes unperceived to all but God, and the celestials who saw these heinous acts for what they were, an opportunity to rid themselves of their Jewish competitors. When John saw the thousands of angels escorting the souls of the dead to Heaven, he smiled. But still, many of the damned were left behind until the second coming of Christ.

From the sky, the horseman Pestilence arrived flying overhead. He drew back his bow and reigned arrows down on the condemned.

Asherah took John by the arm and said, *"Let us leave here."*

When Asherah and John reached their next destination, gunfire was erupting all around them. John heard some men yelling at one another in French. Others were speaking British. He could see their breath as they talked. It was freezing.

"Mother where are we?" John shouted above the shelling of the tanks.

"We are at the Battle of The Somme," Asherah answered John unfazed by the cold or the carnage. *"We are in the belly of The Great War. The War to End All Wars."*

142

It was World War I. The date was November 18, 1916. The French and the British were preparing to mount an attack on the German frontlines. It was dusk, and the only light to be seen were the flashes from the muzzles of the machine guns and the barrels of the tank and artillery brigades being fired from both sides. From the dark John saw a figure approaching he and Asherah. He squinted trying to see who it could be. As the figure got closer, John saw that it was Ariel. The protector of every species of the Earth, except for man, had come because horses were being used as a beast of burden in this battle. German machine guns cut the equine down just as they did the allied soldiers, but unlike the soldiers, the horses had no choice. God had given man dominion over them, and so they died in wars started by men just as horses before them have perished in man's skirmishes. Asherah had been quiet for the most part as She and John observed men dying for a less than noble cause. But when She saw Ariel approaching, She smiled and called to her little one, *"Ariel, I'm here, son."* Ariel ran to her and gave her a hug.

"Mother, it's good to see you," Ariel stopped mid-sentence. *"I mean,"* Asherah put a finger to his lips.

"I know what you meant, My sweetheart," She said caressing his face. *"But go. Do what Your Father has sent you to do. I shall see you back in Heaven very soon."*

With that Ariel and a division of angels that God had dispatched to aid him went about calming the horses and other panicked animals. The German forces continued the barrage of artillery pounding the position of the allied soldiers. The cries for the medics by the British and the French could be heard throughout the trenches, but the fight was far from one-sided. A British captain called out to his men, "God save England." And as a nod to his French allies, he yelled, "They shall not pass!" He climbed up out of the trench, and in that instant, enemy machine-gunfire blew the right side of his head off. His body fell back into the ditch. His death rallying his comrades. The endless artillery bombardment had made the terrain nearly impossible to cross. In the months that the Battle of The Somme lasted, over a million and three hundred thousand men were killed. Also, close to three hundred thousand horses died as well. However, this was the last few hours of the battle, unknown to the allies or the Germans. But what John saw gave him hope for humanity.

"Look, Mother," John said gesturing at a British soldier allowing a wounded German soldier to escape.

As the German soldier nodded his thanks to his British counterpart, Asherah made no effort to look.

"I know, My child. This act of empathy that you see here is a part of God's design."

She didn't explain any further to John. What John didn't know was that the German soldier that had been given a pass was Lance Corporal Adolf Hitler. The future Führer of the Nazi Party and the Third Reich. And while "The War to End All Wars" resulted in the death of seven million civilians, ten million military personnel, and an astonishing eight million horses along with the countless mules and other animals, it would pale in comparison to the sixty million lives lost when the world went to war for the second time in the twentieth century. A war initiated by that very same Lance Corporal Adolf Hitler.

As Asherah and John departed, the multitudes of angels went about the task of escorting the millions of waiting souls to purgatory. As they traveled to what John presumed was the next chapter of The Book of Life or The End of Man, whatever it was to be called, to John, it was all the same-a look at man's short-comings and iniquities. But John, being ever vigilant, was keenly aware that though there were angels at The Battle of The Somme who were working vigorously to usher the souls of the dead soldiers off the frontlines and on to purgatory. The fact that there weren't any demons on the battlefield hadn't escaped his notice, and as an up and coming journalist, it was nagging at him. He needed to know why.

As the wind and sights of times past and present whisked by them, John asked, "Mother, in the middle of all of the chaos, although I saw thousands of angels, I didn't see any demons. One would think if there was any place where you'd see an abundance of the purveyors of evil, as it were, would be smack-dead in the center of a war right?"

"No, My child, you are incorrect," Asherah replied as they continued their ascent or maybe their descent.

For all John knew they may have been standing still. He couldn't tell up from down when they were traversing from location to location.

"The soldiers who bravely fight and die, many are only following the orders of their commanders. The demons who goad the engineers of war are far from the battlefield. They are oft in a comfortable setting alongside the leaders who send young men and women to their deaths as though they are

merely playing a game of war." Asherah looked at John and said, *"But do not be fooled…in war, there are men who are half-demons, and yes, John there are half- angels fighting as well."*

John thought of that British soldier who had spared the life of the German soldier. Before he could ask the question, Asherah answered him.

"Yes, son, the soldier who let his enemy live was half -man, half- angel. Just as the soldier who was given a second chance, was sadly a half-demon," She said with their journey coming to an end.

John looked around, and he knew exactly where they were. He and Asherah were in China. For miles, as far as the eye could see, there were people busy working in the fields harvesting grain and rice, men, women, and any child that was of working age. On the outskirts of the fields massed tightly together, were rows upon rows of stone huts covered by straw rooves. The people wearing tattered clothing worked feverishly as one entity. Some grinding grain into flour, while others, who knew nothing of ironwork, were forced to collect any and all metal objects they could find to toss into small steel backyard furnaces to smelt the metal down and manufacture it into what turned out to be useless, malformed bars of pig iron.

Standing guard overseeing the work being done were armed government soldiers. Their appearance was in stark contrast to that of their countrymen. The folk working the land and manning the furnaces were severely malnourished. No, malnourished is a misleading description. They were skin and bones. Walking skeletons. Those who were too weak to keep stride were beaten to death.

Asherah spoke, *"Come!"* She said emphatically.

From the sky came a black horse. On it sat a burly rider carrying a pair of scales saying, *"Mother for them I bring a quart of wheat for one yuan, and three cups of rice for one yuan."*

The rider dismounted his steed and approached the Queen Mother. John found it ironic that the horseman who brought forth famine would be well, to put it plainly, slightly overweight. As he walked carrying the scales of abundance and lack, the crops of the field dried and withered away under his feet.

"Mother, I am here to return them to our Father. They are near, but they are lost," the third horseman of the apocalypse said kneeling down in front of Asherah.

She placed her hand on his head and told him to rise.

"John, this is Ra͞ebel. His name means they hunger for God."

The three walked through the large village the size of a small city. Asherah explained to John that they were in the province of Hubei. It was 1960 in communist China, and this was the time of The Great Famine. The human suffering that John now witnessed far eclipsed any of the sights that Asherah had shown him prior. Young children sat emaciated in front of several dwellings holding dried grass in their tiny feeble fingers.

"Mother why are these children sitting outside of their homes," John asked.

"These children you see here are being sold in exchange for food."

Asherah's answer stunned John, but then he thought that might be a good thing. A family selflessly taking in another child. Just another example of man's charitable spirit.

"So Mother, although so many are starving, people are still willing to help one another?" John asked, naïve but, optimistic.

Asherah told Rāêbel to take leave and make ready the path for the coming of the fourth horseman.

"Let us see child how generous man is in times of despair."

They walked up the road and into a hut. Hanging by their feet over a pit dug into the ground, gutted and being smoked like wild game or a side of beef were the corpses of two young girls. The father had gone to another province earlier that week and purchased the children from a mother who was near death herself. She could only hope that the man and his family would be able to provide a somewhat better life for her daughters. How could she know that all of China was starving?

The communist regime headed by Mao Zedong had suppressed any news of the widespread crisis. Asherah and John looked on as the wife entered the back room and took the dried and smoked remains of one of the young girls who was no older than four into the rustic kitchen and threw the body on a wooden table. She used a large flat piece of wood to dismember the petite frame.

When the government told all of the farmers to gather all metal articles, even kitchen utensils needed to cook with were melted to help push China into the industrial age. Each family was only allowed to keep a wok to prepare the family's meals. Mao Zedong called it the "Great Leap Forward." What the rest of the west had taken decades to do, he believed he could accomplish in fifteen short years. His unrealistic vision fueled by an insatiable ego crippled China. This time John couldn't stand idly by. As the woman picked up pieces of the young child and threw them into a wok. He charged directly at her, passing through her, he slammed into a wall. With any facade of machismo gone, John sat there despondent and sobbed. Through his tears, he repeated the same question he had asked numerous times before. "Why Mother?"

Before Asherah could respond. Soldiers burst into the home and attacked the father. The family was pleading in mandarin which John understood none of. Asherah reached out and touched John's ear. Their words now translated he could hear the father and mother swearing that they had not stashed away any grain or rice. They raised their hands swearing an oath to Chairman Mao. The same Mao Zedong who had forbidden religion. The same Mao Zedong who had said if half of China's population died from starvation it would be more food for those who were left. But their pledging an oath to a godless dictator paled in comparison to the apathy the soldiers displayed when seeing their countrymen reduced to cannibalism. They were more concerned about making their quota for their respective province, ensuring that they and their families would have ample food rations.

A soldier who appeared to be the ranking officer drew his long saber and lopped off the hand of the father. The other soldiers stripped the mother naked and beat her. They drug her by her hair into the fields in the cold of night and instructed her to work if she wanted to stay warm. After ransacking the family's home and finding no hidden grain, one of the soldiers glanced at the two young children who were tending to their father. He walked over and looked into the wok that contained the now stewing remains of the young girl and snarkily told the father and the children, "Enjoy your dinner," before walking out laughing.

John pulled himself up from the floor. Asherah put her hands together in the hand muff that hung from her waist and said, *"Walk with me, child."*

Outside, there were people stripping leaves and the bark from trees to make soup. Any livestock the government hadn't commandeered had been eaten by the people long ago. Not soon after that, they ate any cat or dog found roaming through the village. John was mortified. He could remember as a teenager growing up how he and his friends would make racist remarks about Chinese eating cats and dogs. At that moment he was disgusted with himself. He imagined if he had a choice between eating the bark of a tree or another human being, would he welcome the sight of a cat or dog being cooked for dinner?

Asherah answered John's question the same as She did previously, or at least some variation of that previous answer, *"The same as it was and always is. Hubris, greed, seeking to be one with God."*

Asherah stopped to stroke the face of a gaunt infant that had been left out in the night's air to die. Mercifully, Asherah delivered the child from its hunger pangs as the infant took its final breath. It had lived a short, misery-filled life, crying for nourishment that never came. An angel came forth and took the child's spirit to Heaven to frolic and play with the other cherubs. Mao Zedong's, "Great Leap Forward" would claim forty-seven million lives, the vast majority starving to death. That is except for the young girls and women who were little more than property. China's second-class citizens, some who were sold, bought and eaten.

INTERVIEWING GOD

Chapter X

Back in Heaven John didn't feel like speaking with anyone. He needed some time alone to sort through his feelings. As he lay on the grass under the evening sky; his arms folded behind his head, he observed the moon ideally placed in the Heavens, glowing incandescently declaring, "Yes the sun is beautiful, but look at me." It reminded John of the marbles he and his friends used to play with as children. John marveled, "How could a God who made such wondrous beauty, be the same God who would let humanity suffer so?" As John lay there brooding, he heard footsteps approaching him. He looked over and saw it was God.

"Do you mind if I join you, My son?" God asked.

"I don't care; you're God. You can do what you want," John responded answering God somewhat indifferent.

God sat down beside him.

"It's glorious, isn't it?" God asked looking up at the stars.

John didn't reply. He had also made it a habit of ignoring God since that night his mother died. He went through life doing what most human beings do when we're hell-bent on doing something we shouldn't. When we hear God speaking to us, we brush it off as butterflies or some other unjustified fear. But this was different. John was snubbing "The Great I Am" to His face. God placed His hand on John's shoulder. John flinched instinctively thinking God was about to take him on another excursion to show him more visions of human anguish. But not this time. This time, God touched John to comfort him. There were no scenes of torture. John wouldn't be made to watch any suffering or punishment being exacted.

God sensed John's dread, and it pained Him.

"You must think Me a monster, My child?"

John sat up, still not saying anything.

God continued on, *"For millenniums I have watched My children whom I created to have everlasting life without sickness or sin, turn their backs on Me for wealth, lust, and power. Some refusing to accept My sovereignty, while others deny My existence. I have looked on as man has maimed and murdered his brother in My name. I have observed as they have hunted My creations into extinction for sport and profit. I and all of Heaven have watched as Man has enslaved his brothers, inflicting great cruelty upon their heads. I have watched hundreds of millions die in wars. I have seen the wealthy amass riches while children perish from hunger. For eons, kings, pharaohs, and emperors go to great lengths to secret away wealth, all for naught. When the graves of those great men are unearthed, there amongst their entombed remains are the riches that could not be carried with them into the afterlife. And now,"* God said with a scowl on His face, *"Some nation's educators are instructed not to mention My name in their schools, but My children are taught how to safely fornicate before marriage?"*

What could John say? He sat there listening quietly. The weight of God's words were starting to hit home. Maybe God was right all along? Perhaps God needed to wipe mankind from the face of the planet and start from scratch .

"Imagine child, if the monies spent on wars were used to feed the hungry. If mankind would selflessly help not only their neighbors but those whom he considers his enemy. I have sent numerous prophets to give men insight of these things, but to what avail? Rulers and clerics elect which of My holy books should be disseminated amongst My beloved." God rose to His feet. *"I watch as fetuses are ripped from the womb. And finally, I lower My head in distress as mankind races towards a nuclear end. Destroying the Earth as he does. So I ask you My son... do you still think Me a monster?"*

John reflected for a moment before answering.

"You're God!" he exclaimed. "Aren't you supposed to know everything before we do it? So if we go about killing, stealing, lying, cheating, sleeping around like a bunch of rabbits and you let us do it, then yes, I guess that makes you the monster."

God could have reprimanded John. Struck him down where he stood, but instead, God painstakingly explained to John what He had told no other before him.

"Yes, I know what mankind will do before they do it. That is why I have given man prophets throughout history to help guide them. Even up until the moment when you commit a sin, I have angels there to urge the soul inside of you to do what is right. You think it is your conscience when it is I, attempting to keep you close to me knowing that all men have the capacity of good and evil dwelling inside of them. No, My child, I am no monster. I am only a father who loves His children unconditionally."

God paused and then said, *"Someone has been waiting patiently to see you."*

John heard her voice before he saw her.

"Johnny, I've missed you so much, honey."

John spun around to see his mother standing there with her arms opened wide. She was just as beautiful as that last day he had seen her. He jumped up and ran to her. Picking her up off the ground as he hugged her.

"Ma' I can't believe it. I've missed you, too," he said through his tears.

God smiled and said, *"I'll leave you two to catch up."*

Lynn Mckinneth curtsied and whispered, *"Thank you, Father."*

At that moment John Mckinneth was that little boy in Kansas all over again.

"Momma'- I can't believe it. I'd given up hope," he said. "I prayed that you were in Heaven, but after awhile I became bitter, and I blamed God for your death."

His mother cradled him as if he was indeed that little boy in Kansas.

"It's alright son. I've been here watching your life the entire time. I saw when you fell off of your bike and broke your arm. I watched when you were fifteen, and you and your friends got drunk behind your Uncle Paul and Aunt Sarah's barn. I saw that night when you read the article about reporters embedded with the military personnel, and you decided that you wanted to become a journalist also. I have been here in Heaven interceding with God on your behalf all along, My love."

159

"Interceding? Interceding on my behalf for what ma'?"

The obvious answer to most parents would be, "Because you're my son, and I love you," but it was more than that. Ever since John was a young boy, he exhibited a capacity for compassion far beyond his years. His inherent ability to empathize with others warmed the heart of his mother. When his father would slaughter one of the chickens, he would come into the house crying inconsolably. Lynn recalled the morning she was preparing his lunch for school. John, who was just six years old at the time, came into the kitchen and asked if she could make an extra peanut butter and jelly sandwich for his friend Max. Max was John's first-grade classmate whose family was also going through some hardships. John noticed during school lunch hour there would be times when his friend Max didn't have any food to eat. Things like that bothered John even as a child. His mother's answer wasn't what he expected.

"Because Johhny, I know now what I've always known. Despite the years of you not wanting to acknowledge God, He's apart of you, and you love Him as much as He loves you."

John hadn't thought of those incidents for years. Max never got the chance to change his life like John had done. His mother and father found him in his room dead from a heroin overdose when he was seventeen. His death would strengthen John's resolve to never get involved with drugs. That was right around the time John was reading the article about an airstrike in Iraq. His mother was correct about that story influencing his decision to become a journalist. But it wasn't the embedded reporters that sparked his desire; it was the thought of the Iraqi children cowering in their homes hearing the U.S. fighter jets roaring towards them. John was determined that his writing would make a difference.

"It's for those very reasons that God has brought you here. He believes that you can help humanity find its way. God has faith that you can save mankind, Johnny."

John didn't know what to make of his mother's words, but if anyone could get through to him, it would be her.

"How mom? I'm just beginning to believe in God again. Why would He choose me? Why not the pope or some politician with connections. At least someone who goes to church on a regular basis?"

His mother laughed the way she used to when he would do or say something funny when he was a child. Her laughter sounded like music to his ears.

"Johnny it's God's way. If you'd read your bible more like your aunt and uncle asked you to, you would know that son." His mother was in full mommy mode. *"God has always chosen people who we think are less than, well, godly. Noah was a drunk, Moses was a murderer. King David was an adulterer, and Paul the apostle persecuted the followers of Christ until his conversion by Jesus. And now our Father who art in Heaven, has chosen my baby boy, someone who thought himself an atheist to save the world."*

John's mother was correct. John was no atheist. How could one hate a God they didn't believe existed.

"But ma', I don't know if I want the responsibility of humanity's existence on my shoulders. I've seen God kill millions because of the mistakes of a few. I've seen children starving and others being eaten because some madman decided he wanted to ban religion. To be honest, I still haven't gotten over His letting you be murdered or His letting millions of innocents die."

John's mother took him by the hand and said, *"Matthew 5:45."*

John looked at his mother and asked, "Matthew 5:45, what does that mean ma'?"

She explained to him as best she could. Just as she had done when he was a young child full of questions.

"He causes His sun to rise on the evil and the good, and send rain on the righteous and the unrighteous. And what that means is this son - while it's true that God punishes the innocent along with the wicked, that's not always the case. Sometimes He afflicts one of our loved ones with disease to draw them and us closer to Him. Other times He brings down natural disasters on nations to evoke empathy from other nations. Then there are the times when we become full of ourselves. We think that because we're making money, living in lovely homes, we're handsome or beautiful, and our kids are doing well in school, we start to believe that all of our blessings are by our own hands, and God, well- He humbles us. I don't have all of the answers son. I, myself would sometimes question how God could let evil people live long and prosperous lives while good folks are cut down in the prime. Children taken before they've had a chance to live at all. And then there are times my love," his mother looked John in the eyes and said, *"A mother will choose to give her life to protect her son. A son who would grow up not only refusing to acknowledge God but despise him as well. And our Father full of mercy and grace will forgive that child and use him to save the world."*

She ran her fingers through John's blonde locks and said, *"You can do this son. The answer has always been inside you."* She squeezed his hand, *"Now get some rest. You have a big day ahead of you tomorrow."*

John held onto his mother. After not seeing her for so long, he wanted to spend as much time with her as possible.

"Ma' will you stay with me tonight?" he asked her.

Lynn McKinneth smiled and said, *"Of course son. You can lay with momma."*

That night John lay beside his mother happier than he'd been in years. But when he awoke at sunrise expecting to see his mother, to his dismay, she had already risen and went to the Hall of Prayers, as did all angels when they weren't watching mankind from Heaven, to listen to the prayers of her and John's loved ones on Earth. On this occasion, it was her sister Sarah and her brother-in-law Paul, who John would soon find out were still trapped in the storm cellar wasting away. Sitting by the fountain waiting patiently, was Sandalphina.

"Good morning brother. Our Father instructed me to let you rest."

John wiped the sleep from his eyes and said, "Thank you, I appreciate it."

He rubbed his hand across his beard which had now grown quite a bit. John unlike everyone else in Heaven was still aging. He walked over to the fountain and proceeded with his morning ritual. When he was done Sandalphina informed him that God was expecting them in the Throne Room. Although John was disappointed that his mother wasn't there when awakened, his outlook was much better that day.

"I'm ready." John said before pausing and saying, "I think."

Sandalphina stood up and extended her massive wings. Fully protracted, they were eight feet in length, and it was indeed an awe-inspiring vision to see her wings outstretched like that of a giant, beautiful, black swan.

"Come, let us go, brother."

The two of them entered the Throne Room which was empty except for Asherah and God who were seated on their thrones talking. John was relieved. He still hadn't gotten over the image of the arch-angels lying prone and begging God for mercy. Sandalphina approached Asherah, bowed and kissed the Queen Mother's hand.

God turned to Sandalphina and said, *"Thank you, daughter. Please leave us now."*

Sandalphina nodded and exited the Throne Room. God and Asherah greeted John, who to their delight now reverently bowed in their presence.

"Good morning, Mother, Father," John said turning and bowing to each respectively. "I'd like to thank you for letting me talk to my mother last night. Seeing her helped me sort through a lot of feelings that I've been dealing with for a long time and..." John stopped and searched for the right words. "And I'd like to apologize to you Father. Apologize for all those years I've hated you. Apologize for the disrespect I've shown you since I got here. But more than that- I want to thank you for your mercy and grace. Thank you for never giving up on me, or punishing me when I clearly had it coming."

God got up from His throne and looked down at John who was still bowing and said, *"Arise My child. You have no need to be troubled. I am your Father, and you will come to understand My infinite capacity to love you when you have children of your own."* God placed His hand on John's shoulder and said, *"And as much as you will love your children, your love for them shall be as but a grain of sand as compared to the love that I, your Heavenly Father has for you and all of humanity."*

God's linen tunic drug on the floor behind him as he walked over to one of the paintings that hung a tad cocked on the Throne Room's wall and straightened it.

"As your mother has explained to you, My son, none who were chosen before you have been what mankind would consider pure. No! Far from it. But I am the God of one thousand, no, boundless chances if it is to be so. And when it is time, My will shall be carried out, just as I decree it. Jonah learned that after spending three days in the belly of a whale," God's hearty laughter echoed in the cavernous room. *"My patience is long-standing, My child. And as you know patience is a virtue."*

John shook his head in agreement. He had grown up hearing his Uncle Paul quote that same phrase repeatedly.

"But that is but one of the Seven Heavenly Virtues," God declared.

John, like many, had heard references made to the Seven Deadly Sins, but the Seven Heavenly Virtues? This was a first for him.

"Forgive me Father, but I've never heard of the Seven Heavenly Virtues," he said.

"Perhaps I am to blame," God replied. *"You see John, once I was disobeyed by Adam and Eve, infuriated,*

I made it known to all of the prophets who came after, and to all of the disciples and apostles of Christ what I found to be detestable. Seven Deadly Sins that would not only make one's life challenging, but would also keep mankind from entering the kingdom of God. But having compassion, I wanted man to have hope, and thus I appointed Aurelius Prudentius, the Christian of Rome, to inscribe a list that would be antithetical to these deadly sins. The first being faith, followed by humility, charity, patience, abstinence, temperance, and diligence. All if adhered to steadfastly, would ensure one's access into Heaven. Regrettably, man would focus on the sin and not the salvation."

God returned to His throne. It was Asherah who now rose from her throne.

She walked over to John and embraced him saying, *"Come, My beloved."*

John wasn't sure he heard right. But yes, Asherah had called him beloved. She too was as compassionate and forgiving as God was. John's sincere repentance had helped to soften Asehrah's guise. She held John close and said, *"Fear not, for the end is near."*

Asherah then began to recite what would be one of the last incantations that John would hear her speak. For this was indeed the end.

"Let us sing to Jehovah, for He has become highly exalted. Let those who have ears hear; Let those who have eyes see! And every creature that is in Heaven and on Earth and below the Earth and in the sea shall tremble at the sight of the Lamb of God who has returned as the Lion of Judah."

When they came to a halt, the two were in the middle of a raging storm. John struggled to hold onto Asherah or else he too would have blown away like much of the debris that flew past them.

The Queen Mother raised her hand and said, *"Wind be still."*

As she did, the howling winds died down around the duo. All about them was total obliteration. That, and the hordes of angels that were wreaking havoc on the planet. Their wings beating furiously whipping the winds that cast cars about like a child's toys and shredded homes like they were mere cardboard boxes. This time there would be no securing livestock or property.

"Mother where are we?" John screamed above the blustering wind.

"We are everywhere on the Earth," Asherah responded. Her answer, like many before, was just another riddle that John had given up trying to figure out. But Asherah wasn't being vague or pompous. In fact, her

answer was rather direct and to the point. Although She and John were in the small city of Portland Indiana, the angels that had come to Earth to end mankind were literally... everywhere! John heard a familiar chant coming from up above. He looked up and saw the figure of the monstrous eagle that he had seen in the Throne Room. It was flying overhead saying repeatedly, *"Holy, holy, holy is Jehovah God, the Almighty, who was and who is and who is coming."*

John and Asherah walked to a church that still stood. That small country church and houses of worship all over the planet had been left unscathed. This too was a part of God's elaborate orchestration. These edifices of sanctimony were now the portals from which the angels that John had seen entering the houses of worship in Heaven came through to execute God's judgment upon humanity. John could hear shrieks coming from inside the building. Asherah, as usual, casually strolled on unfazed by the destruction that was going on around her. Once inside, John froze. He was again forced to witness God's holy retribution. The bodies of the dead who sought sanctuary littered the pews of the church.

The army of Christ loudly repeated, *"Death, destruction, the end of man,"* while methodically slaying demons, half-demons and anyone deemed impure.

Not even the young were spared. Those who weren't killed were left to be judged by Christ who wasn't far behind and would soon be coming. The angels swung their fiery blades cutting down everyone found adulterated by sin while their celestial brothers carried the souls of the dead off to purgatory or the abyss. John didn't know it, but it was now the year 2045, and North America and the rest of the world was experiencing severe unparalleled weather anomalies and natural disasters. The harbinger had been the first major hurricane of the twentieth century that touched down in Galveston, Texas in 1900. Nearly twelve thousand people perished. However, mankind paid no attention to the warning signs. So there would be more to follow, like Hurricane Okeechobee, in 1928. Followed by Audrey, Camille, Agnes and numerous other storms and hurricanes. But the world finally began to pay attention when Hurricane Katrina battered the Gulf Coast of the United States in 2005 slamming sections of Mississippi and submerging close to seventy percent of Louisiana underwater. To their credit scientist tried to warn the world of what they believed to be the next and perhaps the final Mass Extinction Event- the Holocene extinction. An occurrence that would end mankind and life on Earth as we know it! Some world leaders took heed while others ignored the advice of the world's most renowned Climate Ecologist even though, some ninety-seven percent of scientist agreed that human beings were the primary contributor to our untimely end by releasing greenhouse gases into the Earth's atmosphere, deforestation, overfishing, and poaching.

Asherah took John by the arm and said, *"Come."*

This journey would be a short and an entirely different voyage than any of their prior ones. Asherah had taken them to New York City in the year 2025. John found himself in the torch of the Statue of liberty looking out at Lower Manhattan. The view was breathtaking.

"Wow," John said. "I haven't been to New York since I was eleven years old Mother. I'd forgotten how overwhelming it all is," he said.

"Yes! It was grand." Asherah replied.

When John heard the word "was" leave Asherah's lips he immediately knew what was to follow. John braced himself for what was to come as the Queen Mother spoke.

"Keep ancient lands, your storied Pomp! Cries she with silent lips. Give me your tired your poor, your huddled masses yearning to breathe free, the wretched refuse of teeming shore. Send these, the homeless, the tempest-tost to me; I lift My lamp beside the golden door!"

At the age of eleven, John paid no attention to that poem by Emma Lazarus titled the New Colossus, when his Aunt Sarah and Uncle Paul took him to visit Liberty Island. If he had, he would have known Asherah purposely intended to be ironic when She uttered those words that had been written some one hundred and thirty years ago. Words meant to give hope to the multitudes of immigrants that entered the shores of America.

Unfortunately, the waves of newly arriving immigrants of Irish, German, Chinese, Italian and Jewish descent were ostracized and suffered through corrupt racial and economic practices. But the bigotry they endured paled to the racism and brutality that generations of African Americans who were brought to America's shorelines in chains experienced their entire lives.

Yes, Asherah was surely being ironic! As Asherah finished, John could feel the winds beginning to pick up. He looked out in the direction that the wind was coming from. He couldn't see it, but at that moment there were thousands of angels standing atop the waters of the Atlantic Ocean. Their wings churning the deep into a massive deluge that headed toward Lower Manhattan. John could hear the water rushing in from the ocean.

"Mother, what's happening?" John asked in fear for his life and that of every person that was going about their day with no idea it would be their last.

Asherah had no long explanation for John as She had in the past. This trip, Ashera had been deliberately withdrawn. It was as though She was preparing herself for the loss of Her children. Sort of how someone will not want to become attached to a litter of kittens, or puppies that they know they'll have to give away or put up for adoption at some point.

"I have already told you, My child, it is the end," Asherah said stoically.

John couldn't believe his eyes. The water came rushing in like a tsunami. It was almost four stories high. John looked down incredulously. It nearly reached the top of the foundation that the Statue of Liberty rested on. It surged by sweeping up boats and ships that were in the harbor and pushed the vessels over the bulkheads that were built to keep the river at bay. Once the bulkheads were breached, the apocalyptic waters rushed through the streets. Thousands were carried from the Westside of Manhattan to the East River and out to sea. Straphangers packed in like sardines in the subways drowned. It was seven-thirty in the morning. In New York and most of the United States, it was the height of rush hour. The city's streets were filled with people going to work periodically checking their phones for the latest post on Facebook or Instagram. Kids gleefully boarded school buses talking about the new "iPhone 24" that was due out at the end of the week. All dead. To his left John saw thirty- foot waves capsize a ferry full of commuters. The Lincoln, Holland, and Battery Tunnels became watery graves. The New York that survived 9/11 and made it through Hurrican Sandy, the New York that the world had come to know as a bustling metropolis and financial epicenter of the world was gone. Staten Island, Long Island, parts of Brooklyn, Queens, The Bronx, gone!

There would also be lesser known towns and counties that were nearly decimated that many people had never heard of. Places with quaint names like Newburgh, Beacon, Troy, Croton-on-Hudson, and Dobbs Ferry, all gone! Up and down the East Coast from Maine to Florida the death toll was in the hundreds of thousands. Islands in the Carribean were demolished.

The waters came ashore and lambasted their poor infrastructure and second-rate power grids. Islands bordered by the Pacific ocean encountered tropical cyclones and torrential rainfalls, shadowed by mudslides that would kill tens of thousands more.

Asherah took John by the hand and said, *"Salvation We owe to Our God who is seated on the throne, and to the Lamb."*

Asherah had whisked them to India in the year 2054. There were millions, perhaps trillions of flies and maggots feasting on the dead bodies of those who had succumbed to famine and disease. John was witnessing the walking dead in real life. India had been leveled by a succession of super-typhoons.

"We are in the City of Varanasi. These are the riverbanks of the once holy Ganges river, My son."

"Holy river?" John thought. "How could this cesspool be considered holy?" he said to himself eyeing the riverbank peppered with trash and rotting corpses lying about.

Dogs wandered up and down the banks of the Ganges feasting on the rancid and decaying flesh of the deceased while goats and cows fed on the garbage. Not far from where they were standing human feces and cow dung floated by. A few yards upriver John observed factories dumping chemicals and a variety of dyes into the water. The river, this holy river – was befouled! Adding salt to the wounds, India was in the midst of a drought, giving many of its residents no choice but to drink the foul water. Those who gave in to their thirst were infected with the bacteria "Giardiasis." A nasty parasite which caused hundreds of thousands of cases of diarrhea amongst the populous city. In the Western world, diarrhea was curable, even laughable. In the third world, it could be fatal!

"Mother," John said, "If the river is considered sacred then why is it so, well... dirty?" He asked, disgusted.

"It is because men are foolish. They are still not aware that they are connected to the Earth and all that is on the Earth, My son," Asherah said.

Perhaps John knew what Asherah was alluding to. Maybe he realized that the corrupt Indian government could have spent the money decades earlier to have the Ganges cleaned up but chose to line their pockets instead. Whatever the reason, at that moment- John had an epiphany. He began to grasp the fact that sin, big or small was the root cause of what ailed humanity. Whether it was destroying the planet, genocide or a something as trivial as a little white lie. Whether you

177

believe in God or the devil, who could deny that mankind is greedy enough to do anything for wealth and power, and prideful enough that he would ignore any advice contradictory to that end! The fracking, offshore drilling, hunting animals into extinction for their ivory, destroying natural habitats and overfishing of the world's oceans, nothing could get between man and his fortune. So what if our children and their children's children would have to foot the bill. And yes, John was correct in his assumption. But he had overlooked an unwritten sin. That character flaw that God declared the eighth deadly sin, "Apathy." What John and so many were remiss in recognizing are the little things that are taken for granted. People in developed countries leave the highest carbon footprint, driving automobiles that hasten global warming and climate change. Leaving the lights on in rooms that we're not occupying. And why not? We can afford it, or so we think. Taking those thirty-minute showers wasting up to a hundred gallons of water. John felt himself becoming uncomfortable again. As well he should. He was guilty of all of those offenses. The long showers. Letting the water just run while washing dishes. Though, like most, John tried to justify his wasteful habits. He told himself he had no choice but to drive everywhere he went, right? Hardly anyone walked or road bikes anymore.

Asherah turned to John and said, *"It is time for us to take leave, it is almost finished."* She embraced John and said, *"Come forth he who has been given authority over the Earth and Earthlings, to kill with a long sword and with food shortage and with a deadly plague and by the wild beast and pest of the Earth. Stars shall fall from the Heavens and make fire upon the Earth. Lava shall spew forth into the sea killing every living thing; And God Himself will cause the Earth itself to quake, to give aid to Him who sits upon the pale horse!"*

This was it! The day of reckoning that prophets, disciples, apostles and holy men for centuries have been heralding. At the beginning of the twenty-first century, the doomsday theorist were coming out of the woodwork forewarning anyone in earshot that the end was near. Who could 've guessed they were right? The hideous semblance of the Eagle traversed between North America, Europe, and Central America causing floods where there would be floods, earthquakes where there would be earthquakes, volcanic eruptions where there would be volcanic eruptions, and so on; Mudslides, landslides, droughts, wildfires, heat waves, disease, and famine. In Central America, South America, Africa, and the Middle

East - the Bull, the second of the monstrous quartet was also wreaking havoc. Entrenched in Asia, the Middle East, and Australia, were the Man and the Bull! And while the Bull, the Eagle, and the Man had numerous brigades of angels to assist them in their task, and the trio all worked in concert to wipe mankind from the face of the Earth, the Lion was sent alone before them to the Arctic and Greenland at the beginning of the new millennium. His three companions would be dispatched shortly after.

The Lion of the apocalypse, not to be mistaken for the Christ Jesus, "The Lion of Judah," was tasked to walk the frozen tundra in solitude, inhaling oxygen and exhaling methane gas from his beastly nostrils. Slowly, gradually, warming the Earth's atmosphere, melting the ice sheets and the glaciers of the Arctic. To the layman, this was far less nefarious than what was now taking place in the rest of world. But to the Climate Ecologist, Environmental Scientist, and Conservationist across the globe this too was cause for alarm! For not only would it contribute to the seas and world's oceans rising at catastrophic levels, but eventually the Arctic would dissipate and become a point in history in which humanity would denote as the beginning of the end. As for the naysayers that cited the expansion of

Antarctica's sea ice and those who decried global warming as a hoax- Antarctica would be next!

When the politicians and the power brokers of the world and those who backed America in pulling out of the Paris Climate Agreement realized their folly, it would be too late. The collapse of world governments, deterioration of branches of law enforcement, and many nation's militaries stretched beyond capacity resulted in mass looting, assaults, rape, and murder! Civilization or any similitude of law and order was nonexistent!

The little things that so many had come to take for granted were gone. There would be no going to the doctor for that back pain or running to the supermart for milk. Gas stations were sparse. When it was found out that one of the few remaining gas stations would have fuel, riots broke out. Eventually, whenever an owner would get fuel, he'd have to pay armed guards to help maintain order. Pharmacies and supermarkets were some of the first retail outlets that were looted. Painkillers were sold for ridiculous amounts of money as did aspirin, cough medicine, and simple toiletries. Those with food and no guns were robbed or killed. Sometimes both. Groups of any law abiding citizens that were lucky enough to survive banded together for protection. The streets, like that of the river banks of the Ganges, were littered with the dead. Millions fled from the cities and towns into the wilderness. The rich and poor all hid and sought Jehovah God!

Their final destination to John's surprise was home! He and Asherah were back at his Aunt Sarah and Uncle Paul's farmhouse. An angel stood beside the storm cellar holding the reigns of a pale horse. His face was contorted and sullen.

Asherah called to him, *"Maveth, I am here, My beloved."*

He was "The Fourth Horseman of the Apocalypse." The one men called death. His twisted face belied the sadness in his eyes. Maveth had been there from the beginning when Cain murdered Abel. Before that day, he was full of joy and yes, life. Happily watching Adam and Eve in the Garden of Eden along with all of the other angels Heaven. Now, ever since, for ages, Maveth and his legion of angels have been there as men, women, and children take their last breath. This time he was here for John's aunt and uncle.

The tree limb that had broken off and knocked John unconscious had fallen on top of the cellar and gotten wedged under the lip of the siding on the house. When Sarah and Paul first heard the tree fall on the cellar doors with a loud thud, they tried as best they could to open them. When that failed, they reasoned that their nephew Johnny would be coming back soon. The two of them waited as minutes became hours, hours became days and days became weeks. Perhaps if John's uncle hadn't been injured, he might have found a way to force the doors open. But neither he nor Sarah could muster the strength to free themselves from what would become their grave.

John ran past Asherah and Maveth. He kicked loose the tree limb and opened the cellar. Immediately the putrid scent of death emanated from the storm cellar. John crept down the three steps and saw the skeletal remains of his loved ones. He cried out in agony, "No! Please, Mother, No. God, No!"

It was all he could do. There was nothing left of his aunt and uncle to hold. It was as God said. There are no time constraints in Heaven, a day in Heaven could be years on Earth. Alas, John's aunt and uncle had been dead for months. They had only brought enough food and water for two to three days. Five days after the last drop of water was gone they died of thirst and dehydration.

Asherah walked to John and comforted him saying, *"They did not suffer, My son. God saw to it that they died peacefully praying as they perished."*

Asherah's words did little to give John solace. The thought of his aunt and uncle in the cellar starving to death and dying of thirst would be something that would haunt him for the rest of his life.

As Asherah took John's hand, She turned to Maveth and said, *"Go and wait for the Christ who is coming to battle the enemies of God who are on the Earth which is now called Armageddon."*

Maveth took leave to meet Jesus in Africa. The battle for the souls of men would end where it started.

Asherah pulled John close and declared, *"O You kingdoms of Armageddon cry out to Jehovah; The war chariots of God are innumerable- Let His enemies be scattered, And let those who intensely hate Him flee and be returned unto the dust, for the Son of man, has come to save that which is lost!"*

Chapter XI

Asherah and John's journey ended with them back in the garden. Asherah headed to the palace leaving John standing there. There would be no mention of his aunt and uncle nor any uplifting words from her to help him deal with their deaths. While it was true, Asherah had been sympathetic towards John at times, to say She kept her emotions close to the vest was an understatement. If he had to sum it up, John would have to say at best Asherah was stoic when it came to her dealings with him and mankind. Frankly, although God made light of the power that the "Word" wielded, John's gut feeling told him Asherah was to be feared.

He looked up and saw his mother who had just exited the palace walk past Asherah and bow. John slowly walked over to his mother contemplating how he would break the news to her that his Aunt Sarah and Uncle Paul were dead. Even at a time like this, John ever selfless was more concerned about how his mother would feel.

"Hi, mom, it's good to see you again," John said forcing a smile.

Just as he was about to break the news to her, she cut him off.

"I know son. Are you okay?" she asked kissing him on the cheek.

"I'll be alright ma'. But Uncle Paul and Aunt Sarah... Why ma'? Why did God let them die?" John wiped a tear from his eye. "They were two of the most God-fearing, God-loving people that I ever met in my life ma'."

How could John's mother tell him once again that everything was all a part of God's plan? He was just beginning to recapture his faith. Telling him something like that could turn him against God forever. Lynn McKinneth looked around to see if anyone was near.

She leaned forward, with her lips next to the ear of her only child, the child whom she gave her life for that night fifteen years ago and whispered, *"Johnny nothing that the Queen Mother has shown you in the future has happened. You can still change it son. You can save the Earth, humanity, your Uncle Paul, and Aunt Sarah. You only have to find a way."*

Before Lynn Mckinneth could say anything else, Sandalphina came flying from the sky with a sword of fire in her right hand. She had just returned from

Armageddon. She and John's mother greeted one another.

Sheathing her sword Sandalphina turned and addressed John, *"Our Father has need of you in the Throne Room brother. Please follow me."*

John's mother kissed her son goodbye and said, *"I love you, Johnny. Remember son- you can do this."*

John hugged his mother not knowing it would be years before they would see one another again. In the chamber of the Throne Room, no throne sat empty. Not only were Asherah and the archangels seated upon their respective thrones, but to John's surprise, so were Christ and Satan! The scriptures were correct. Satan could travel to and from Heaven to converse with God as he pleased. He used places of worship as portals to go back and forth just as the angels did. The Almighty was the first to speak.

"John, My son, you have been made aware that the end of days has befallen mankind. But I, and I alone against the counsel of My wife Asherah and My son Jesus saw fit to spare you from the day of judgment and bring you here to Heaven to reside with your mother if that is what you want. If you decide to return to Armageddon, then you shall face the same fate as the rest of humanity. The choice is yours, My child."

The decision to save one's self or face an inevitable death was a no-brainer. But the words that John's mother whispered to him, *"Nothing that the Queen Mother has shown you in the future has happened,"* and *"you can still change it, son,"* reverberated in John's psyche. That and the image of his Aunt Sarah and Uncle Paul's wasted corpses in the cellar. John knew what he had to do. He would have to try and change the mind of the Holy Trinity.

"Father, Mother, Lord Jesus you've shown me things that made me sick to my stomach, while at the same time I was horrified seeing what human beings did to one another. So I understand what brought us and by us, I mean you all to this point," John said looking at the three of them as he spoke. "But before I give you my answer, I ask that you consider all the acts of benevolence that humanity has done."

Jesus sat there with His gold helmet on His lap listening quietly as John spoke. He then held up His hand and asked John, *"What good has man done that would wash away thousands of years of wickedness? As we speak the angels are looking down onto Armageddon watching men and women being beheaded. Animals are slaughtered for greed and children are sold into slavery for immoral purposes. And e'en if none of these things were occurring, man is still destroying Armageddon!"*

Jesus's voice rose as he made it clear that there would be no reprieve from the sentence that had been passed down. From John's left came a voice on his behalf and that of mankind.

"One moment, brother," the voice said addressing Jesus. "Let's not be so quick to rush to judgment. Let the boy speak. What harm can it do?"

It was Satan. John didn't know it, but Lucifer had just as much to lose as humanity. With the coming of the Apocalypse, it would also bring about an end to his rule on Earth.

Asherah cut her eyes at Lucifer and said, *"Hush, Yacubiel. This is not the time nor place for your insolence child."*

Satan said, *"Yes, Mother."* before slumping down and saying nothing more.

It was as John suspected and Asherah declared, She was undeniably just as powerful as God! Yes, Satan had dared to challenge God's authority, but it was the "Word" of God that cast him out of Heaven and onto the Earth before finally sentencing him to Sheol. Fortunately for John, Satan's shenanigans had brought him more time.

"I can admit that as a species we have flaws, but what about the good that so many of us do?" he asked pausing for a second.

Every eye in the Throne Room was now looking at John waiting to hear what he would say next.

He went on, "We have organizations all over the world that are dedicated to saving the planet, helping the underprivileged, the sick and the disenfranchised. Those same organizations that you showed me earlier, like Green Peace, The World Wildlife Fund, Doctors Without Borders, and The Children's Fund, these are just a few that I can think of off the top of my head, but really, there are so many foundations out there doing their part; I just can't name em' all. And what about the everyday heroes that again, you yourselves have acknowledged? The firefighters, the soldiers, and the police officers? Or, the neighbors who go out of their way to comfort someone in need, doesn't that count for anything?" John asked looking around the Throne Room.

God and Asherah remained silent, but Jesus Christ who had once given His life for mankind was now man's prosecutor. Jesus had walked among men as Immanuel (God is with us). He remembered going off

190

to pray in the wilderness and returning to find the disciples asleep after He asked that they keep watch. Jesus recounted how He was greeted with cries of "Hosanna" on the Sabbath and days later that same crowd was calling for His death. He knew better than John that man was flawed, but this was the Son of God. There was no vengeance in His heart, only what was just. Jesus, like His Father, still loved mankind, but man would be cleansed from the planet once again, it had to be done.

"Yes, We have observed these organizations who do indeed provide charity to the poor, but the heads of these establishments are compensated handsomely. Some are paid hundreds of thousands of dollars for their so-called good will. And of those who give, they cannot wait until their taxes are due to collect on their contributions. I know more than anyone that man is inherently self-serving."

As Jesus spoke, John could hear the chants of *"Death, destruction, the end of man."* The angels of Christ had resumed their battle cry. Their mantra now louder than any previous time before. John could feel the opportunity slipping through his fingers. He was stumped. Had he failed?

As John thought of what to say, Jesus sat his helmet on the floor and got up from His throne and declared, *"It is finished!"* He looked at John and asked him, *"What will you do brother? Do you choose to stay and reside here in Heaven or return to Armageddon and wait for My arrival?"*

This was it. John had to make a choice, Heaven or Earth, or rather Armageddon as it was now called. As Jesus had stated in the bible, either hot or cold, There could be no in-between. If only John had just a little more time. He was sure that he could think of something profound to say. Who would have thought that a Journalist would be at a lost for words? Yet, this was the predicament that John found himself in, hot or cold. John knew the choice he had to make.

He opened his mouth and yelled out, with as much audacity as he could muster, "Neither!" John dropped to his knees and said, "I choose death!" He looked around the chamber and said, "Father, Mother, and my Lord, I ask that you take my life in return for the lives of my aunt, uncle and for the lives of as many of the innocent that you think my life is worth."

He then prostrated himself at the foot of the throne of God as the archangels had done. The Throne Room grew hushed, and the chanting ceased. The Messiah sat back on His throne, and turned to the Heavenly Father who smiled and clapped His hands.

"Well done, My son!" God then looked at Asherah and said, *"I was right again, My love."*

Asherah nodded her head in agreement and said, *"Yes, My love, you were again correct."* And She too smiled.

The archangels stood and thunderously applauded. For John's life was not only worth that of his aunt, uncle, and the innocent but for all of humanity as well. His selfless act had saved mankind.

Sandalphina approached John with her wing's fluttering enthusiastically and said, *"You did it, brother! You have done what no other has done besides the Son of God Himself."*

John had the look of a deer caught in head-lights.

"What? What did I do?" he asked Sandalphina oblivious to what had just transpired.

"Through your willingness to sacrifice your life brother, man will be given more time to find the path from which they have strayed,"

Sandalphina explained to John that while many had given their lives for their loved ones, friends, and even strangers, only he and Christ had been chosen to do so for all of humanity. God motioned for John to come forward. He touched John and instantly John's countenance was restored as it was upon his first arriving in Heaven.

God then said, *"Your work here is finished, My son. But before you depart, know you this; The day of reckoning is at hand and you are tasked with spreading the word about the things that you have witnessed here in Heaven, and of the things that you have seen that are to come in the future."*

John accepted the responsibility, and he swore an oath to God that he would tell anyone who would listen to the things he'd witnessed.

"Father, you have my word. I'll do my best to inform every nation on the planet that we must join together to stop global warming, the senseless killing of animals and the destruction of the planet. If not, the end is imminent."

John thanked the God and kissed the hand of the Queen Mother.

Before he left, he hugged Sandalphin and said, "Thank you for everything sister."

God, Asherah, the archangels and Jesus wished John farewell and sent him back to Earth. His mother Lynn walked to the entrance of the palace where God and the rest of the celestials stood and kneeled.

"You did well, My daughter," God said telling Lynn Mckinneth to rise.

It was as St. Peter told John upon his arrival at the river crossing, *"In Heaven, there are no secreted thoughts, only truths."* Those words that John's mother whispered in his ear, *"nothing that the Queen Mother has shown you in the future has happened,"* was too a part of God's omnificent composition. A morsel of information given to nudge John in the right direction. No matter how wayward, if man called on Him, God would always be there for His children. God smiled thinking of John's act of altruism and the good that man was still capable of. But that smile soon faded, and it was replaced with a look of scorn.

"Michael, Uriel, escort Lucifer to the Garden of Worship and see him off - back to Hell," God said coldly.

The two archangels drew their blades and said, *"Let us go, brother,"*

Satan said goodbye to God and Asherah, but before leaving, he turned to Jesus and said, **"I'll see you soon on Earth, brother."**

The Messiah didn't bother to respond. He knew all too well the snares of His fallen brother. Satan had tried to persuade Him to betray God ever since He was a young child. Then as now, Lucifer was no match for the

Son of God. When they met on Armageddon, the Christ would be ready for war!

John's journey came to an end where it all began. He was a few feet away from the storm cellar. Blood trickled down the left side of his forehead as he ran over and pried the tree limb free from where it had gotten wedged under the house. He opened the cellar doors and saw his Aunt Sarah applying pressure to his Uncle Paul's wound. "Thank God you guys are okay!" John said climbing down the stairs after picking up the medical bag that was lying where he dropped it.

"We're fine Johnny, but we heard something crash on top of the cellar."

His aunt looked and saw the blood that was starting to dry on John's head.

"Oh my, Johnny. What happened to your head, honey?" she said gently flicking John's hair to the side to get a look at the small gash."

Let me tend to your Uncle Paul, and you're next boy. I don't know what I'm going to do with the two of you?" Sarah declared taking the bag from John and grabbing the gauze bandages out of it. "When your Uncle Paul and I tried to push the doors open they were stuck. We weren't at all worried though. We knew you'd be right back son."

John looked at the house, which except for the busted doors and the mess inside, was in pretty good shape. The storm had passed over the town causing minimal damage. After his Aunt Sarah got Uncle Paul bandaged up and took care of the cut on John's head, the three of them piled into John's truck and headed to the hospital. His Uncle Paul had surgery to reset the bones in his wrist. The doctor took a look at John's wound and ordered an MRI and a CT scan to be on the safe side. John had suffered a mild concussion, but the doctor said he would be fine with a couple of days rest.

When they returned home and got settled in, John began telling them the fantastic story of his going to Heaven and meeting God, Jesus, the archangels, and God's wife, Asherah. While his aunt and uncle were both fascinated and delighted that John believed he had gone to Heaven and met with the Almighty, they said the storm lasted no more than twenty- minutes, and by John's own account he was in Heaven for more than a week.

As faithful as John's aunt and Uncle Paul were, they attributed his belief that he'd been to Heaven as hallucinations caused by the concussion. It was the same story that Christ faced in His hometown of Nazareth. Many of His neighbors who watched Him grow up as a child refused to acknowledge Him as the Son of God, declaring, "Is this not the carpenter's son?" John was disheartened, but He wasn't delusional. By no means did he think he would come back to Earth and everyone believe the tale he was recounting, but he thought for sure his aunt and uncle would believe him.

Resolute, John asked his boss, Mr. Conley, if he could run the story in the "Clay County Caller." Mr. Conley took John inside his office and told him that he thought he should take an indefinite leave of absence until he got himself together. John cleared out his desk and left. As he did, he could hear the whispers of "Poor kid. That clunk on the head messed him up good."

That night John got down on his knees and prayed to God and Christ for answers. The answer John received wasn't one he expected. God told him he would have to travel across the country from state to state, city to city and town to town. Just as the disciples and apostles had done in days of old.

Early the next morning John awoke before sunrise and packed his bags. He left a note on the kitchen table thanking his aunt and uncle for being the best parents any kid could hope for. John also told the two of them that he could never repay them for their love and generosity and that he loved them both so very much. He climbed into his pick up truck and left Clay County and his aunt and uncle's farm, tears rolling down his face as he did. John had made a promise to God, and he was determined to keep his word. John traveled the country working odd jobs making enough money for food, gas, and a place to bed down for the night. Staying in one place long enough to attend the local church, synagogue, temple or mosque in whatever town or city he happened to stop in. Other times he would park his truck on a busy street and break out a cardboard sign and shout word for word the story he had told his family and boss.

God, Christ and the Word were going to destroy mankind before we destroyed the planet. Most people assumed he was crazy. Eventually, the local authorities would show up and run him off, citing that he was disturbing the peace. John would jump into his truck and hit the road again. That road brought him here to New York, and that's where I met John Mckinneth.

I encountered him standing on a corner in Upper Manhattan with that cardboard sign that read, "The End Is Here!" While he looked a bit worse for the wear, I didn't get the sense that he was abusing drugs or was someone who was suffering from mental issues. I stopped and took note for a moment. I don't know, maybe it was God, but a feeling came over me compelling me to listen to what this young man was saying. His story was beautiful at parts and terrifying at others. Midway through his tale I approached him and offered to buy him lunch. He hesitated at first, but when I confessed to him that I felt as though God wanted me to hear his story, he smiled and accepted my invitation.

As we sat and ate, he began to tell me the most remarkable tale that I've ever heard in my life. I asked would he mind giving me his account in detail and he agreed. After days of meeting up and hours on the phone, I had enough notes to help him carry out his mission. I gave him my word just as he had given God his word. This story is the end result of that oath. I'm going to go on record and say, "Yes, this story sounds absurd." You can believe it or not, but according to John Mckinnneth, we can do away with racism, war, genocide, hunger, poverty, and prejudice, but if we don't begin to reverse the effects of global warming, deforestation, and a host of other crimes against the Earth, you, me, and the rest of humanity are doomed!

INTERVIEWING GOD

I.Y. WADE

Made in the USA
Columbia, SC
24 June 2018